FAMILY
SECRETS

*Five extraordinary siblings. One dangerous past.
Unlimited potential.*

Zach Ingram—A dead ringer for his adopted brother, the hunky economics professor knows his kidnappers have the wrong man. But can he entrust his life—and heart—to the psychiatrist who was sent to hypnotize him?

Maisy Dalton—The leading hypnosis expert quickly finds herself falling under the spell of her patient's piercing blue gaze. But can she believe his wild tale that they're both in grave danger…and need each other to survive?

Jake Ingram—Adopted at age twelve, the financial whiz has no memory of his childhood. But when a letter arrives informing him his life is a lie, can he put the pieces together in time to save his brother and uncover the secrets of his past?

Agnes Payne and Oliver Grimble—The evil duo helped genetically engineer the Extraordinary Five—children with superhuman abilities—more than thirty years ago, only to lose them in a fiery accident. Or had they…?

About the Author

MAGGIE SHAYNE

is a veteran author with more than thirty novels to her credit. It takes a lot to get her excited about any story, but when she was invited to write the lead novel for the FAMILY SECRETS continuity, she got very excited. At first glance the premise seemed groundbreaking; then she got the rest of the details and knew her first instincts had been right.

Maggie has always favored stories that break the mold and deliver the unexpected. She's written about vampires and witches, psychics and shamans, fairies and time travelers. But nothing she had dipped her pen into before seemed quite like this series idea. It wasn't quite paranormal. Closer to science fiction, though, she suspected, maybe not so fictional. It was one of those ideas that rests well within the realm of the possible, and that's far more unsettling, to Maggie's way of thinking, than the realm of the impossible. It makes the reader pause, to wonder, "What if…?"

"What if…?" is a question Maggie Shayne has never been able to resist.

Coming next from Maggie Shayne, *Thicker Than Water,* from MIRA Books this fall. Visit Maggie on the Web at www.maggieshayne.com.

MAGGIE
SHAYNE

ENEMY
MIND

Published by Silhouette Books

America's Publisher of Contemporary Romance

Special thanks and acknowledgment are given
to Maggie Shayne for her contribution
to the FAMILY SECRETS series.

 SILHOUETTE BOOKS

ISBN 0-373-61368-7

ENEMY MIND

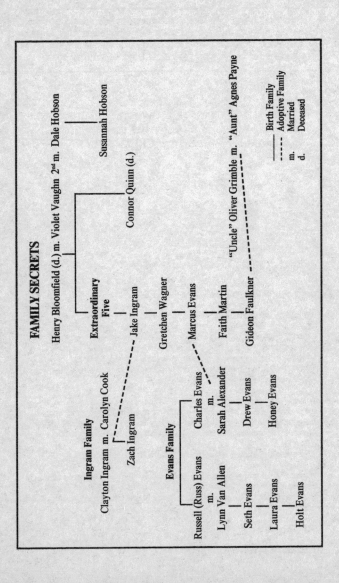

FAMILY SECRETS

Henry Bloomfield (d.) m. Violet Vaughn 2nd m. Dale Hobson

Susannah Hobson

Extraordinary Five

Connor Quinn (d.)

Jake Ingram

Gretchen Wagner — Marcus Evans

Faith Martin

Gideon Faulkner

"Uncle" Oliver Grimble m. "Aunt" Agnes Payne

Ingram Family

Clayton Ingram m. Carolyn Cook

Zach Ingram

Evans Family

Russell (Russ) Evans — Charles Evans
m.
Lynn Van Allen   Sarah Alexander

Seth Evans   Drew Evans

Laura Evans   Honey Evans

Holt Evans

——— Birth Family
- - - - Adoptive Family
m. Married
d. Deceased

One

There was no spring in his step when he walked out of the Tanner Lecture Hall at Greenlaurel University and into disaster. Students, some of whom were freshly rested, having napped through his class, seemed to respond to the early spring sunshine, the warmth in the air. They were smiling, bright, laughing, holding hands as they strolled around the Texas campus.

He didn't stroll or smile or laugh. He sighed, as bored with his life as his students were with his lectures, and walked down the concrete steps to the parking lot and his very practical, very serviceable silver-gray Ford Taurus. For the money he'd paid, the car was the most dependable car on the market, according to his research. So what if this particular model hadn't come with too many extras? Who needed extras? It had A/C, a cassette player and power windows. No power locks. No sun-roof. No cruise control. No CD. Heck, he might have preferred one or two of those options, but for the money, this car was perfect.

He stuck the key in the lock, turned it and opened the door. As he did, a deep-throated roar caught his attention, and he straightened up to look. A handsome young jock cruised by in his Porsche Boxster, gleaming cherry-red, with chrome so shiny it reflected the sunlight and nearly blinded him for a moment. The radio was blasting, and a gorgeous coed sat in the passenger side.

The driver waved. "See you next week, Professor Ingram."

"Have a good weekend, Derek," he replied with a wave.

For a moment, just a tiny moment in time, Zach Ingram felt something stir in his belly, something a little like envy, but mostly, a dull yearning. He shook it off and told himself that he was the consummate boring professor. He was not a jock. He wasn't macho. Women would occasionally give him a second look, but rarely a third. It wasn't that he was unattractive, he supposed. He and his brother looked so much alike people were constantly getting them confused, and his brother attracted women like honey attracts bees. But his brother was tough and masculine, athletic and adventurous, bold and intimidating, not to mention considerably wealthy. A real hero type.

Zach was...well, just Zach. He wasn't sure how he'd perform in a crisis, since he'd never had to. Jake was always there to jump in, take charge.

Sighing, Zach got into his car, fastened his seat belt and started up the engine. But just as he went to put the vehicle into reverse, another car drove up behind him and stopped. He couldn't back up without smashing right into the driver's door of the blue sedan. And the driver, a harmless-looking woman of perhaps sixty, very frail, with a thin face, sat there staring at the steering wheel and shaking her head.

Pressing his lips together, Zach got out and walked around behind his car, and up to hers. "Ma'am, is there something I can help you with?" he asked.

"Oh, dear, I just don't know what's wrong. It won't go."

He smiled just as little as he glanced in at the controls. "You've got it in neutral," he told her gently. "Just move the shift a little to the right."

She lifted her brows in surprise. "Oh, my! How silly I feel! Dear young man, would you mind doing me one more favor?"

"Of course not, ma'am."

"Just open that back door for me, if you don't mind."

"The back door?" Zach glanced at the rear door on the driver's side.

"Yes, that one right there. Would you open it for me?"

Shrugging, he moved to the back door and opened it, expecting it to stick or something, but it opened easily. He stood in the opening, glancing into the back seat.

"Oh, that's so much better," the old woman said. "Now if you'll just get into the car."

"Get into the—" He glanced up at her as he spoke, then stopped at the sight that greeted him. The sweet little lady had a handgun and she was pointing it at him.

"Get in," she said.

It was a prank, he thought. It had to be some kind of fraternity prank or something. It couldn't be real.

But then he felt a looming presence behind him, and even as he turned, there was a jab in his thigh. He'd been stabbed!

But no. It wasn't a knife. It was a hypodermic needle. And within the time it took for him to realize that, Zach's head was swimming and his knees had turned to water. He sank slowly, and the large, blond-haired man behind him shoved him into the car, got in beside him and slammed the door. Then the lady drove.

The last words he heard came from the old woman as she said, "Just relax now, Jake. Everything's gonna be just fine."

Dr. Maisy Jane Dalton was sealing a very large envelope, sighing in contentment at a job well done and looking forward to her first free afternoon in six months, when the telephone rang.

She closed her eyes and told herself to let the machine get it. She'd been working for more than a year on her second book. The first, *Hypnosis and Memory: An In-Depth Perspective,* had been acclaimed as a breakthrough work on the subject by the entire psychiatric community. This new one, *Deprogramming the Human Mind,* had been eagerly anticipated, and for a while she'd been sorely afraid she would never get it done by her publisher's deadline. But as of today, as of about an hour ago, in fact, it was finished.

The telephone rang again.

She needed time off. All she wanted to do today was go to the Austin post office, drop the envelope into the outgoing mail and take the rest of the day, followed by the rest of the month, maybe, to just let her brain rest.

The phone rang a third time.

Then again, she thought, it was probably better to keep her mind occupied. Less time for regrets that way.

Sighing, hoping it was nothing even remotely work-related—like another talk show appearance or print interview or government agency in search of a consultant—she picked up the phone. "M. J. Dalton," she said.

"*Dr.* M. J. Dalton?" a woman asked. "The psychiatrist?"

Older, Maisy thought. And she sounded nervous, under stress. "Yes, that's me."

"Oh, thank God! You've no idea how relieved I am to hear your voice. Dr. Dalton, I am in desperate need of your help!"

Maisy frowned. This was sounding less like a business-related call and more like a frantic patient in need of a session. But everyone knew she didn't see patients anymore. She consulted with those who did, wrote books and articles about subjects on which she'd been hailed an expert, and delivered the occasional lecture. But she did *not* work one-on-one with patients. She tried to avoid doing anything one-on-one with anyone, in fact. "What is it you think I can help you with, Ms....?"

"It's my nephew. My darling, precious nephew. He doesn't know us, doesn't even know who he is anymore! Oh, you have to come. You're our only hope, Dr. Dalton."

Maisy bit her lip, frowning at the phone. "I don't work with patients anymore, Ms....?"

"Smith. Agnes Smith. And I know. I read that you had retired from private practice, but I'm hoping you'll make an exception. This is a desperate situation, Doctor."

Maisy drew a breath, calmed her mind, didn't allow herself to answer until she'd first thought her answer through, planned it in advance. "If you can tell me a little bit more about the situation, Ms. Smith, I'm sure I can refer you to someone for help."

The woman sighed, disappointment heavy in the sound. "He's been living on some sort of compound, with one of those cult groups you hear about."

"Which one?" Maisy asked, her interest rising. Cults and their mind-control tactics were a particular area of interest for her.

"Which one? My God, how can that matter? The point is, we got him back. We...*took* him back."

She winced inwardly, knowing what that meant. "You had him abducted against his will?"

"We didn't see that we had any choice in the matter, Dr. Dalton. We love our nephew. We wanted him back. Those people, they—they brainwashed him. He doesn't even know us anymore." She was crying now, sniffling softly in between her words.

Maisy nodded, understanding the woman's motivations, sympathizing with them, even while pitying the poor boy who'd been so traumatized. "How long was he there?" She'd picked up a pencil, begun making notes.

"Years," the woman said. "He vanished from the family more than a decade ago, and we only recently learned where he was. We have no way of knowing how long he's been there."

"And how old is he now?"

"Thirty-five."

Maisy stopped writing, the pencil point pressing into the paper. "Thirty-five?"

"Yes. Why, is that a problem?"

"I...no. I'm just surprised. People in this situation are usually a great deal younger."

"We brought him home to our ranch three days ago, Dr. Dalton, and we thought he would come around when he saw familiar things, but he hasn't. We don't know what to do."

Maisy nodded, sighing. She couldn't deny being intrigued by the case. A thirty-five-year-old man undergoing mind-control techniques for a period of years would be an incredible challenge.

But her self-installed safety features kicked in to

tell her to stay out of it, to pass the case to someone else, maybe advise the doctor by phone or e-mail, but not to get involved on a personal level. She liked the safe haven of her home office. She liked the impersonal distance she kept between herself and the outside world. She worked in solitude, spoke to crowds of strangers from a podium or, even better, through the pages of her books. That was as close as she cared to get.

She was a psychiatrist, and she was not prone to self-delusion. She knew why she'd chosen to withdraw from the world after the loss she'd suffered. It had been a conscious decision, made three years ago. When she was ready to emerge from her carefully woven cocoon, she would. But she wasn't ready. Not yet.

"Dr. Dalton?"

The woman's voice jarred her from her musings. "Yes, I'm here. I was just going through some names, colleagues of mine who might be able to help you."

"I don't want any of your colleagues, Dr. Dalton. I want you."

"I'm sorry, but—"

"I did my own research," the woman said, her voice pleading. "I know there is no one in the business who is as knowledgeable about mind control and deprogramming as you are. You're the best, Dr. Dalton, and we need the best. Every other doctor we've contacted has told us to get you. You are our only hope for restoring our darling Jake's memory."

She licked her lips, lowered her head, prepared her refusal in her mind. "Ms. Smith, I—"

"Just come out here, Doctor. See him, just see him, just once. If you don't want to take the case, then I'll accept that, but at least see him. See for yourself why we're so desperate for your help."

It *would* be fascinating, a little voice inside told her. Just to see this patient, this rare case. It wouldn't mean she had to take it herself. And it might give her a clearer picture of what was going on, so that she could refer the man to the best possible deprogrammer for his particular situation. She allowed those thoughts a hearing in her mind, weighed them and measured them.

"Can you bring him in?" she asked at length.

"No. No, it's impossible. You'll have to come here." The woman began rattling off driving directions, and Maisy scribbled them down automatically, before realizing that she hadn't flat out refused.

By the time the woman finished, Maisy had made her decision. She wasn't sure it was the right one, but she trusted her inner feelings, had learned to hear them and follow their guidance. Once, they'd guided her to back out of society. Now they were gently urging her to step in again, just a little bit. Maybe only for a quick peek. Hell, she had a free afternoon, anyway. She wasn't sure if she wanted to go out there because this promised to be such an interesting case, or because it was simply time for her to make this move. But she found herself saying, "All right. I'll see him. But that doesn't mean I'll treat him."

"Thank you. Thank you, Dr. Dalton."

Maisy glanced down at the directions. "How far is this ranch of yours from Austin?"

"Two hours. It's quite a drive. But it's a lovely place, and we have extra rooms if you decide to stay over. Aside from seeing Jake, you might think of it as a mini-vacation. Can you make it tonight?"

Maisy pursed her lips, glanced at the completed manuscript in the envelope, waiting to be mailed, looked at the four safe, comforting walls of her office surrounding her, and then at her clock. Three p.m. "I need a couple of hours to get things squared away here. If I don't get lost, I should be there around seven."

"We'll set an extra place for dinner. Thank you, dear. Thank you so much. For the first time since our Jake came home, I have hope."

Maisy hung up the phone, closed her eyes and wondered if she was ready for this. Picking up the large envelope, she walked from the office into the living room of her home. She'd planned to pour a glass of wine, sit outside on the deck and enjoy the April afternoon, maybe read the newspaper and just relax.

Through a set of sliding glass doors, the deck stood empty, the redwood patio furniture beckoning. The newspaper lay untouched on the living room coffee table. She glanced at the headline, Renowned Economist Jake Ingram To Aid Feds In Investigation Of World Bank Heist.

She hoped there would be progress reported in that particular case, since the repercussions it had caused in the financial world had sent her stocks plummeting to near nothing. She'd lost most of what she'd put away for retirement, as well as Michael's life insurance money. Still, there was no time to read the paper in search of a ray of hope for the world's economy and her own future. Not now.

Sighing, she picked up the newspaper, folded it in half and tucked it under her arm. Maybe there would be time later on to relax and catch up on current events.

She headed upstairs to pack an overnight bag, just in case.

Jake Ingram sat at his desk, wondering if he really was as good as everyone seemed to think he was. He'd been tapped to help the government track down those responsible for the biggest heist on record—the robbery of the World Bank. He wished for a moment that bank robbers would stick to the old-fashioned methods: burst in with guns and demand cash from tellers, or break in by night and crack the vault. But no, these bank robbers were far more sophisticated. The money had literally vanished overnight, through a spiderweb of computer transfers so complex it would take a genius to figure out where it had finally ended up.

Unfortunately, the genius chosen to do just that was him.

He hoped to hell he could live up to his reputation, but even for Jake, this was a challenge. The wedding would have to be postponed…again. God, Tara was going to be heartbroken. It occurred to him, just briefly, that he probably should be, as well.

The afternoon mail sat unopened on his desk, and he turned to it, knowing full well he was procrastinating. He had two equally daunting tasks to face: plunging headlong into the investigation and breaking the news to Tara. Taking a quick peek at the mail seemed more appealing than either.

He flipped through envelopes filled with tragic-looking stock market analyses, even worse financial reports, updates on how the world was responding to the knowledge that its most sophisticated and secure bank's computers had been accessed by criminals and robbed of a staggering amount of money.

Everyone was panicking, pulling funds, selling stocks. If the World Bank wasn't safe, nothing was.

Suddenly, he stopped flipping through the mail. There was one small envelope addressed to him in a handwritten scrawl. No return address, no postage stamp. Odd. He buzzed his assistant, and the young man appeared almost instantly. Fred was an up-and-comer, a near genius with numbers himself.

Jake held up the envelope. "Where did this come from?"

The younger man eyed the envelope and straightened his glasses. "Found it under the office door when I came in this morning." Then he held up a newspaper. "You made headlines again today. That's four days in a row now."

Seeing his name emblazoned across the front page, Jake sighed. "I told the feds to keep my involvement quiet, but apparently they either ignored that advice or sprung a leak. By now the entire world knows I'm on this case."

"You think that's a bad thing?"

"I don't think it's a good one."

Fred tilted his head. "You need anything else?"

"No, go on." When Fred left him alone again, Jake opened the envelope, and a scent wafted from it as he did. It was oddly familiar. Violets. It smelled like violets. For a moment his stomach clenched into a knot and his throat tightened as if with emotion, but he had no idea why. He quickly forced those feelings aside and continued examining the envelope.

It contained a single sheet of lined paper covered in the same spidery script that was on the envelope.

Dearest Jake,
Everything you believe about yourself, about your life, is a lie. There are things in the past, things you don't remember—things you've not been allowed to remember. But now the time has come when you must know the truth about your past. Who you are. Where you come from. You could be in grave danger, Jake. It's time to ex-

hume the buried past. Try to remember, Jake,
try! It's more important than you know. I'll help
you to find the truth. I'll be in touch soon.

The letter was signed with a single initial, the letter
V.

Jake sat there staring at the note for a long time,
willing more information to appear on the page, but
of course none did. He licked his lips. It wasn't for
real. It couldn't be for real. There were very few people in Jake's life who knew about the secrets that
plagued him most, the secrets of his past.

But they were secret only to him. He remembered
nothing about his life prior to his adoption by the
Ingram family at the age of twelve. Nor was there
anything sinister about it—his birth parents had been
killed in a car crash, and his young mind had been
unable to deal with the trauma of their loss. So he'd
blocked it out. It was an extreme reaction, but a plau-
sible one. It happened sometimes, the doctors told
him.

But that didn't make it any easier not to remember
being eleven, or ten, or nine. Not to remember his
elementary school years, or any of the friends he must
have made then. Not to remember learning to ride a
bike.

But worst of all, not to remember his own parents.
His birth parents. It felt as if he was betraying them
by forgetting them, when they had given him life and

raised him all those years. But there was nothing left of them in Jake's mind or memory. Nothing.

His adopted parents and his adopted brother, Zach, were the only people who knew about the post-traumatic memory loss and the pain it caused him. They were the only people who knew about the odd dreams that sometimes haunted his sleep. And they wouldn't have told anyone else. He trusted his family beyond question.

But *someone* knew he didn't remember his past. Somehow, someone else knew. And whoever it was, was trying to use that information now—to what end, he couldn't imagine.

Or maybe he could, he thought as his gaze slid to the newspaper lying on his desk, proclaiming his involvement in the investigation of the biggest robbery in recorded history. Maybe he could.

Two

Agnes Smith's ranch, Maisy deduced after two and a half hours of driving, must be in the middle of nowhere. She didn't know what Texas county she was in by the time she reached what she hoped was the right place, much less what town. The final turn on the list of directions took her onto a dirt road so narrow she hoped she wouldn't meet any oncoming cars, because there wouldn't be room enough for two to pass. No signs. No lights. Nothing but a dirt track winding through thick trees and the occasional open field gone to seed.

It was dark, and she was thinking seriously about turning back, when the tunnel of woods ended abruptly at a scraggly lawn that looked in need of water and a farmhouse that looked in need of paint. Lights glowed from the windows, though, and the driveway was a welcome sight. She didn't really care if she had the right place or not at this point. She needed a break and a chance to get her bearings. And maybe a telephone. Any port in a storm, she thought as she pulled slowly into the worn dirt drive. Her car's headlights illuminated the clapboard house, its square, four-paned windows and its slightly sagging front porch. This couldn't be the right place, she thought. Agnes Smith had said she'd done her research, so she must have some idea what a private consultation with M. J. Dalton would cost. The people who lived here could never afford her.

Maybe they hoped to play on her sympathy and convince her to donate her services. Evidently they'd done more research than Maisy thought, and knew she was a pushover for that kind of tactic.

She shut off the engine and opened the door, turned and set her feet on the ground.

A huge dog lunged out of nowhere, all teeth and noise. Rapid, earsplitting barks and deep, echoing growls, combined with rapidly snapping jaws and a spray of saliva, made her heart hammer in reaction, even as she jerked her feet inside and slammed the car door closed again. The beast stopped just before reaching the car, teeth bared as it continued to bark. Then she saw the tightly pulled chain that was attached to the collar around the furry neck, and she traced it to the far end where it was attached to a dead tree. A ramshackle doghouse stood under the tree.

Okay. It couldn't reach her. As long as the chain held. She slid across the seat, never taking her eyes off the dog, thinking it might be best to slip out the passenger side. Or maybe just start the engine and leave, if she hadn't been shaking too hard to drive. When she reached for the passenger door, it opened all on its own.

Her gaze jerked upward to meet pale blue eyes in

an aging male face, and she had to bite her lip to keep from yelping in alarm.

"Dr. Dalton?" the man asked.

With one hand pressed to her chest as if she could manually slow her heartbeat, Maisy nodded, because she didn't think she was capable of speaking.

"I'm sorry to have startled you, Doctor. I'm Oliver Smith. Agnes and I have been expecting you."

He stood there holding the door for her. She took a breath and told herself he was not a frightening looking person. In fact he had a rather placid and nonthreatening face and a welcoming, if nervous, smile.

She slid out of the car, got to her feet and straightened her clothes. "I wasn't sure I had the right place." She extended a hand. "It's good to meet you, Mr. Smith."

As he took it, gave a shake, his was chilled. Like holding raw meat.

"Don't mind the dog, now," Mr. Smith said. "He's all bark, no bite."

"I don't think I'll put that to the test, if you don't mind." She said it with a smile, but her heart still skipped a beat when she glanced back at the animal. It was a mongrel, with the distinctive black-and-brown markings of a rottweiler, but a longer, narrower face and long floppy ears.

It stared back at her, not even blinking, it was so focused. It had stopped barking now, but it leaned forward, keeping its chain and collar pulled so tightly she didn't know how it could breathe, much less growl the way it was. The animal's entire body quivered with pent-up rage.

Then the front door of the house creaked open, and Maisy glimpsed the woman standing there. She could only see her in silhouette—curly hair close to her head and a body so thin it appeared frail.

"Bring her inside, Oliver, before that foolish dog of yours scares her to death."

"He wouldn't hurt a fly," Oliver said, but he obeyed even as he spoke, taking Maisy's elbow and gently guiding her toward the front porch. He gave the beast a wide berth, giving Maisy the idea that he was more afraid of the dog than he was letting on.

"What's his name?" she asked as they climbed the four front steps.

She didn't think it was a difficult question, but from the look Oliver shot the dark-haired woman in the doorway—who had to be Agnes—he was having trouble with it.

"It's Rufus," Agnes answered. "I swear, Ollie, have you been forgetting your vitamins again?"

He only looked at her blankly.

"He keeps arguing that there's no medical evidence supporting the claim that ginko biloba improves the memory, but it certainly couldn't make it any worse. Come in, dear. Come in." The woman stepped back, holding the door open.

Maisy walked into the farmhouse and looked around. The living room was not large, not fancy.

Judging from the lingering odor, it had been freshly painted. The brown carpet was spotless, and the sofa and chairs looked new. The upholstery was a floral print except for one overstuffed chair, which was brown. The curtains in the windows matched the floral pattern.

"I want to be clear on one thing, before you see our Jake," the woman said.

Maisy turned to face her, surprised at her rush to get to the subject at hand without even a pretense of small talk. Agnes's hair was dark and her face was narrow and stern. She didn't like the woman's tone. It was rather imperious. Rather commanding. Hardly the tone she'd used on the telephone when she'd all but begged Maisy to come out here. Hardly the tone of a simple rancher's wife.

"We don't expect you to treat him," Agnes said, rushing on the moment she was assured she had Maisy's attention. "We're not asking you to be his therapist or his counselor, much less go digging into any *issues* at all."

The word *issues* was filled with so much sarcasm, Maisy thought the woman must doubt there were any such things.

"We just want you to unlock his memory. That's all."

Frowning hard, Maisy almost snapped out a retort, but she stopped herself. What was the point? She'd only promised to see the man once. She wasn't going to be the one treating him.

"Mrs. Smith," she said, speaking slowly and with deliberate calm, for which the woman ought to be grateful given that she'd been driving forever and then attacked by a vicious dog. "Whoever ends up helping Jake will have to be free to proceed as they see fit, and as they feel is best for the patient. You're not going to be able to dictate Jake's treatment. You should probably get used to that idea."

Agnes frowned, and for a moment, Maisy thought she would argue, but then she seemed to reconsider. "I don't suppose there's any point in discussing it now, before you've even seen him." She pursed her lips. "I'll take you up to him now." Then she turned, marching through the living room and up the straight, narrow staircase.

Maisy, left with little choice, marched up behind her, then down a long hallway to a door at the far end.

Agnes opened the door. Maisy stepped inside, looked at the man lying in the hospital bed, which must have been purchased just for him, and felt the reaction in every part of her body: shock, anger, pity and something else, something far too odd and unidentifiable to examine just now.

He lay on his back in the bed—asleep or unconscious, she wasn't sure which. His thick, black hair was a mess and his face was shadowed by a few day's growth of whiskers. In spite of the tousled hair and unshaved face, he was a strikingly handsome man.

The odd little feeling got a little stronger, twisting

around uneasily in her belly and whispering in her brain. She couldn't hear what it was saying.

The man in the bed tugged her closer without opening his eyes. She'd seen good-looking men before and never felt the urge to run to them. It wasn't his looks pulling the tides in her body the way the moon pulls the ocean. It was the helplessness that got to her, she guessed. It roused her protective instincts.

"Why is this man tied down?" she asked, and she knew her tone was sharp.

Another man, blond and big as a mountain, rose to his feet. Maisy had been so compelled by the man in the bed that she hadn't even noticed the other one, sitting in the chair nearby, as if keeping watch over the patient. "It's not their fault," he said in a deep, but deliberately quiet voice. "He's been violent. Tries to attack anyone who comes near him."

She frowned at the man, doubting him.

He thrust out a hand. "I'm Bob," he said. "Jake, here, is my cousin. We were practically raised together, before he vanished." As he spoke, he gazed past her, toward Agnes, who gave him a nod as if of approval.

Maisy shook his hand briefly. "I'm Dr. Dalton," she told him, pulling her hand free almost immediately and moving closer to the man in the bed. He wasn't at rest. His body jerked every now and then, his arms twitching spasmodically against the ropes that held him. Maisy leaned close to him and spoke softly, her tone deep and level. "Hello, Jake. My name is Dr. Dalton. I'm here to help you."

She touched his forehead, noting the clamminess of his skin, the light coat of cold sweat. Beneath his closed eyelids, his eyes moved rapidly.

"I'm here to help you," she repeated. "I'm going to help you. All right?"

His eyes opened suddenly, and he speared her with an electric-blue gaze so potent it was jolting. "Help me."

The power of his eyes when they locked with hers and the plea in his voice combined to rock her right to the core. She trembled down deep and had to resist the instinctive urge to pull away from such a powerful force. Dammit, she hadn't worked with patients in far too long. She was nowhere near ready for this.

But her own feelings were unimportant here. She had to think of the patient. "Yes. Yes, help you. I've come to help you," she told him.

"Help me," he repeated, breathing faster. Her hand rested near his on the bed, and suddenly he closed his around it. "Please…"

Then he closed his eyes again, and his on her hand relaxed. Relaxed, but remained. She looked down at his hand on hers, the fine mist of hairs at his wrist, the redness surrounding the tight rope at his forearm, the pale tan line where a wristwatch used to be.

Leaning closer, she slid her hand from his, only to close it on his wrist, feeling for his pulse. She found the beat and counted while looking at her own watch.

Then she turned to the others in the room. "Have you been medicating him?"

"Of course not," Agnes said. "He's been like this since we found him."

She frowned, because it made no sense. Then she went about the business of untying the ropes at his wrists and ankles.

"You really shouldn't be doing that," Agnes said. "He'll run off the first chance he gets."

"Oh?" Maisy looked up. "I thought you said he was tied down because he'd been violent."

Agnes narrowed her eyes. "As you'll find out the first time he's lucid and you're close enough that he can land a blow. Running off is yet another reason."

"He's not going to run off," Maisy said. "He's not able to, not in this condition." She untied the ropes. "He should be in a hospital."

"No. No, I'm not letting him go. Not again. And since I'm his closest living relative, and he's not in sound mind right now, it's my decision to make."

She was right about that much, Maisy thought, amazed that she was as informed as she was about the legalities. But she licked her lips and turned to face the older woman. "I can't treat him if you aren't going to do what I think is best for him, Mrs. Smith."

"Just try it my way first. If he doesn't begin to improve immediately, then we'll reconsider." Agnes moved across the room to a bedside stand, leaned down and opened the drawer. She withdrew a book, a children's book of nursery rhymes, which she handed to Maisy. "This was his favorite when he was a little boy. He'd make me read it to him over and over, night after night, until he fell asleep. I know this will help trigger his memory."

Maisy held the old woman's gaze until her tears spilled over, and then she couldn't look anymore. She pursed her lips, lowered her head. Agnes Smith was brusque one minute, pleading the next. But she was clearly beside herself over seeing this man, who must have been like a son to her, reduced to the state he was in right now.

"I will do whatever you recommend, Dr. Dalton. I give you my word on that. But you can't possibly make a decision with no more than a glance at him. Please, spend some time with him tonight. We have a guest room ready, and we made extra for dinner. Jake's already been so traumatized, I don't think he could bear another move, another strange place and a whole new set of strange people around him. I think it would push him so far over the edge we might never get him back." She touched Maisy's arm. "If you do decide he has to go, surely we can take him in the morning. It's dark outside now. He gets so much worse at night. I can't bear to put him through such an ordeal at night."

Maisy sighed, feeling truly sorry for the woman. The look in her nephew's eyes, the desperation in his plea, kept replaying in her mind. And Agnes did have a point about the trauma of moving him again, particularly if he had issues with the darkness. She looked at the people around her. "Bob, is it? Would you mind getting my bags from the trunk of my car? There's an overnight case and a smaller black medical bag."

Bob glanced at Agnes, who nodded just once, then he rushed out of the room. When he was gone, Agnes lingered. Maisy didn't care. Her attention was once again on the patient.

"I'll have him put your bags in the guest room," Agnes said.

"Just the overnight case. I need the medical bag in here." She spoke without looking up. She was looking at the patient's eyes as she gently lifted his lids.

"We held dinner for you. If you'd like to join us—"

"What are you having?" she asked, still not looking.

His pupils were unnaturally dilated, Maisy noted. Then she sank her fingers into his thick, dark hair, probing his scalp for cuts or bumps or any signs of a head injury.

"Fried chicken, mashed potatoes, gravy—"

"No, that's not going to work. Your nephew is becoming dehydrated, and I'm not sure yet, but I wouldn't be surprised to learn he's been using psychotropic drugs, some of which might still be having an effect. We need to flush his system with clear fluids. Water, broth, ginger ale, gelatin, any of those sports drinks would be ideal. They're high in electrolytes." She sighed, shaking her head slowly. "Ideally, we'd start an IV. We'll have no choice but to hospitalize him if he can't take sustenance by mouth—"

"Oh, he can. He can, truly," Agnes said.

"Yes, I've seen him eat, too," Oliver interjected, speaking for the first time. "He's not like this all the time, the way you see him now, I mean. Sometimes he's almost normal."

Maisy nodded, but doubted she would agree with the man's take on "normal." "There should be water and other liquids on hand constantly," she said. "We need to keep him drinking.

"We'll get some right now. And don't forget this," Agnes said before she left, patting the book she'd left lying on the bed. "I know it will help. I know it."

Maisy frowned as she watched the woman go. There was no way she could treat this patient here. He needed to be in a hospital. But so long as his vital signs were good tonight, she supposed she could wait until morning to break it to his family.

The pretty one had come to help him, his fogged mind told him over and over. She'd said so as she had run her warm, soft hands over his body. She'd held his hand, his wrist, run her fingers through his hair. Doctor. She'd said she was a doctor. And that was good.

She didn't look like a doctor. She was too soft, and she made him think of mink, with her huge round eyes the color of mahogany wood, and her brown satin hair, all twisted up at the back of her head. Mink. Smooth, satiny mink.

"Jake, I need you to wake up now. Just a little, just enough to drink, okay?"

That voice. He loved that voice. He'd stopped responding to the demanding voices of the others, especially that of the old woman, who kept insisting that he remember the past, and reading him nursery rhymes as if he were a toddler.

Her voice, this new voice, he loved. It soothed his frayed nerves like honey. He would go anywhere she told him to go. Do anything she told him to do. So he forced his eyes open and shifted them until he found her face. His vision cleared slowly and he focused on her.

"There, that's very good, Jake."

His mind sent the words to his lips. *No, I'm not Jake. I'm Zach.* But he heard what his mouth did with the message and it wasn't pretty. It emerged as something approximating, "Nah Jay." And he was pretty sure he drooled as he spoke, but he couldn't help it.

God, he had to talk to this woman, he had to tell her—

"'Nah Jay'?" she asked, holding a straw to his lips.

He obediently opened his mouth, closed it on the straw, tried to suck down the water. God, he was thirsty. The water hit his mouth, but his throat closed automatically, and he choked.

The angel—that's what she had to be, an angel—

took the glass away, rolled him onto his side and rubbed his back until he could breathe again. Then she lowered him to his back once more.

"It's all right. Just a little at a time. You have to go slowly. All right?"

He tried to nod, not sure if it worked or not.

She returned the straw to his lips. He tried again. Once he convinced his mouth and throat and lips to work together, and the flow of water had begun, he kept it going, drinking and drinking and drinking.

When he came up for air, he had to suck it in rapidly. His lungs were thirsty, too.

"Easy, now," she said. "My goodness, you are thirsty. And Agnes was right, you can take liquids. That's very good, Jake."

"Nah Jay," he managed again.

She blinked down at him.

"Nahht," he told her, emphasizing the T sound at the end. "Jay."

"Are you trying to tell me your name is not Jake?"

Sighing in relief, he let his eyes fall closed and nodded his head.

"I see. You've got some other name, then?"

Another nod. He tried to say it, to tell her his name was Zachary, but he couldn't make a coherent Z sound. All that came out was spittle when he tried. He made the effort again and again, until she smoothed a hand over his cheek, where there might have been a tear of frustration. He couldn't be sure.

"It's all right, don't get so agitated. It's going to

take some time, but you'll be all right. You'll be able to talk to me, and you'll be able to remember everything you need to. I promise you that. I swear it.''

He closed his eyes, sighed softly, gave her a nod, even though there was nothing wrong with his memory. These people seemed to think there was, and she only knew what they had told her.

''I'm the best there is at what I do. I'm going to help you. I want you to believe that.''

He forced his eyes open again. God, she was beautiful. His salvation, he thought.

''I don't want you to be upset,'' she said, ''I want you to stay as calm and relaxed as you possibly can. That's going to help me help you. All right?''

He nodded at her. She stroked his hair again. He loved the way she touched him—often and repeatedly. ''Just to contribute to that state of calm, I'll stop calling you Jake, since it obviously upsets you.''

He sighed, nodded.

''But I have to call you something. No, no,'' she said, when he tried to form the sounds that made up his name. ''No. You'll tell me when you can, and it won't be long. Don't fight for it, just let it come naturally. And until you can tell me what name you prefer, I'll just make up my own name for you. Okay?''

He tried to smile, but wasn't sure if he managed it.

''Now, how about some more water, Handsome?''

That time he knew his smile worked, because she returned it to him.

''Oh, you like that nickname, do you? I thought

you would. My husband used to like that one, too."
She replaced the straw at his lips, and he sucked down
more water. Then the woman set the glass aside and
brought a soft cloth to his chin to dab it dry.

"There now, Handsome. That's enough for now.
You're exhausted. Why don't you take a little nap?"

She backed a step away from the bed. Moving
more quickly than he had realized he still could, he
closed a hand around hers and held on. She looked
down fast at him, locking onto his eyes, and he tried
like hell to send her a message.

"I'm not going to leave you," she told him. "I'll
still be right here when you wake up. I promise."

Thank God, he thought. Thank God. He was saved.

Three

Why, she wondered, had she promised him that she would stay? It meant she couldn't get out of here. Not tonight, anyway. Then again, she realized she wouldn't have made the promise at all if she hadn't already decided, on some level, that she was spending the night here.

She had made that decision the second he'd opened his eyes and looked into hers. She didn't really *want* to get out of here, and she knew it. She should. She had expected to be eager to head back home, to hand this case off to a colleague, but she wasn't. And she was sorely afraid it was for all the wrong reasons. Her practical side argued that this was a fascinating case, a once-in-a-lifetime opportunity to study a patient like him. Her ethical side argued that she could help this man, and that she had no right to walk away from him and risk his well-being because of it.

But her emotional side—the side that wasn't even supposed to exist anymore—told her loudly and clearly that she wanted to stay because of those beautiful, tortured blue eyes and the way her belly knotted up when they locked with hers.

There was a tap on the bedroom door. It opened

immediately after, and Bob walked in, carrying her medical bag. For the first time, she took a good look at him. He was a tall man, strongly built, and probably close in age to Jake. "We can have dinner whenever you'd like to come down," he told her. "Ag— my mother has heated everything up for us."

Maisy nodded, opening her bag, and pawing through it. She located a serology kit, removed the cellophane wrapper.

"What's that you're doing?" Bob asked, coming closer, leaning over her shoulder to watch.

She found a vein in her patient's arm, swabbed it down. "I'm going to take a blood sample so we can figure out what kind of drugs he's been given."

He frowned. "Drugs?"

"It's obvious he's got something in his system. At least I'm ninety-nine percent sure of it."

"You can do that, just with what you have in your bag?"

She glanced up at him, but only very briefly. "No, not here. I'll have to take the sample to the nearest hospital with an on-site lab, back to Austin if there's nothing closer, and leave it. I imagine it will take at least a day to get any results." She inserted the syringe into the patient's arm, noting the involuntary flexing that resulted from the brief stab of pain. Then she removed the rubber band from his bicep and let the blood flow into the tube on the end of the needle. "Do you know if he was going by any other name while he was with this cult?" she asked.

"You mean like Moonray or Rainbow?"

She sent Bob a sideways glance, caught his teasing—and perhaps flirtatious?—smile. "It's good that you've kept your sense of humor, given the gravity of the situation."

His smile faltered. "I'm trying, but it's not easy. I'm worried about him. We've been like brothers."

Bob had pale blue eyes, the color of glacial ice, full lips and closely cropped blond hair. His neck was as big around as her thigh, she thought. He looked like a Nordic marine. It was hard to see past his size to his real concern for his cousin. He looked too tough to be hurting or worried, and probably, she reasoned, was in the habit of hiding emotions rather than parading them around for all to see. Making jokes and flirting with the doctor were likely his most familiar coping methods. She shouldn't hold it against him.

"I promise you, this is going to get better," she told him. "We're seeing your cousin at his worst right now. Once the drugs have had time to clear out of his system, he'll be more lucid, and we can really do some work with him." She withdrew the needle, holding a tiny gauze pad to the injection site, and then bent his elbow over it. "Hold his arm up for me, will you?"

Bob nodded readily, taking Jake's wrist and keeping his arm bent.

Maisy removed the tube from the needle, labeled it and set it aside. Then she applied an adhesive strip to the tiny puncture in Jake's arm.

"Ready?" Bob asked.

She glanced up at him, then back at her patient. She hated to leave him, even briefly. But she did have to talk to his family, tell them of her decision and her plan of action.

Her stomach growled to remind her that it wouldn't kill her to get a bite to eat, either. And the blood sample would need refrigeration until she could get it to a lab for analysis. So she nodded, picked up the test tube and followed Bob down the stairs.

He started to pull the door closed after they'd both exited the room. She put an hand on his huge shoulder. "Can we leave it open, so I can hear him if he wakes up?"

Holding her eyes with his, he shook his head. "Not while he's alone. He could get out of the bed, fall down the stairs. Anything could happen." He closed the door and slid home the bolt on the outside. It was shiny brass, and around the screws that held it in place were twisted bits of pale, aromatic wood. The lock had been recently installed, probably just for poor Jake. Maisy couldn't argue with the wisdom of the idea, but she didn't like it, either.

Swallowing her distaste and willing her patient to remain sleeping for at least a few minutes, she followed Bob down the stairs and across the Spartan living room. There was no television, she noted for the first time. God, what did they do around here for entertainment?

Tempting scents assaulted her, distracting her attention, and she picked up her pace as she followed Bob into the kitchen.

Agnes was just setting a platter of fried chicken on the table. There were a huge dish of steaming mashed potatoes, a boat of gravy and a small bowl of mixed vegetables. There was a cutting board with freshly sliced, warm-from-the-oven bread and real butter.

"This is incredible. I hope you didn't go to all this trouble just for me."

"Don't be silly, Doctor. We're ranchers. This is the way we always eat," said the bone-thin Agnes as she took a seat at the head of the table.

Maisy licked her lips, glancing at Oliver, who wasn't carrying a spare ounce of fat, either. The considerably larger Bob, she supposed, might very well eat like this all the time. He wore jeans and a plaid shirt with the sleeves rolled up to his elbows. His clothes looked new.

"So, then, this is a working ranch?" Maisy asked, still standing.

"Oh, not anymore. Not really," Agnes said. "We got rid of the cattle long ago, except for a few of the best breeders. We sell a handful of calves every year, and we still board a few horses to help pay the taxes. The ranch has dwindled to a couple hundred acres. But it's enough. It's plenty, actually, for just us."

"And about all one man can handle by himself," Bob added with a smile. He shrugged. "Maybe now that Jake is back…"

He didn't finish. He didn't have to, for the **hopeful**

glance he sent to his parents, and then to Maisy, spoke volumes. Although there was something off about it. Perhaps the way it vanished the moment Agnes nodded in agreement and turned her attention to rearranging the platters on the table.

"Have you decided anything, Dr. Dalton?" Oliver asked softly.

Maisy nodded, walking slowly to the refrigerator and finding a safe, clean spot to set the tube of blood she'd drawn. "Yes. I'm going to try to treat your nephew myself, rather than handing the case off to a colleague."

"Oh, thank heavens," Agnes said.

Maisy closed the fridge, washed her hands at the sink, then went to take her seat at the table. "I'm going to have to leave in the morning, but not for long. I drew some of Jake's blood, and I need to take it to the nearest hospital for analysis."

Bob nodded. "She says it'll tell her what sorts of drugs he's been given," he explained to his parents.

"I see," Agnes said. She helped herself to a smidgen of mashed potatoes and passed the bowl to Maisy. "Oliver and I have to leave in the morning, as well."

Maisy looked at her questioningly.

"Family emergency," Agnes explained. "We shouldn't be gone for more than a few days at most, but…" She frowned hard, as if in thought. "Well, no matter. I'm sure Bob can handle Jake all by himself for a few hours."

"More like for half the day," Bob said, "if the

doctor has to take that blood all the way back to Austin.''

''Austin?'' Agnes asked. ''Is that where the blood sample needs to go?''

Maisy nodded. ''Unless you know of a hospital lab closer?''

''No, I'm afraid I don't.'' Agnes passed the platter of chicken without taking a piece. ''But Oliver and I have to drive right past Austin. We could deliver it for you.''

Maisy tilted her head to one side, considering the offer. She hated like hell to leave the man upstairs alone. She was sure Bob's concern was genuine, but she didn't see him as the coddling type. He wouldn't see anything wrong with leaving the patient locked in his room, or tied to the bed, while he went out to see to his duties around the ranch. And that would only traumatize poor Jake all the more.

''I could give you a letter to take along, ordering the tests I need performed. I could even call ahead and let them know it's coming.''

Agnes nodded. ''It really would make more sense than taking that long drive needlessly.''

Maisy nodded. ''You'll need to keep the sample cool on the way.''

Bob snapped his fingers. ''I have a small insulated cooler, just the right size to hold a six-pack and a little ice.'' He got up and went to a cupboard, rummaged around inside and pulled out the box, holding it up. ''Would this work?''

"It's perfect." Maisy added a spoonful of mixed vegetables to her plate of food. "I'll write the letter tonight, so it'll be ready for you first thing in the morning. And I'll give them a call after 8:00 a.m., so I can speak with the lab tech who'll be on duty when you arrive."

"You've thought of everything, dear," Agnes said. "I can't tell you how grateful we are." She rose from the table and left the room. She came back with a fat white envelope, which she laid on the table in front of Maisy.

Maisy frowned at it.

Agnes said, "If it's not enough, just tell us. We'll pay anything to get our Jake back."

Cash. The envelope was thick because it was stuffed full of cash, she realized as she picked it up and peeked inside. "My goodness. This is... unorthodox, to say the least."

"We prefer to use cash whenever we can. It's a quirk of my husband's. Never did trust banks. Is it a problem?"

Maisy studied the woman's pinched face and tried to quell the niggling feeling in the pit of her stomach that something was wrong here. "No. No problem," she said slowly. There was one, but she wasn't sure she could put her finger on exactly what it was. Suddenly, though, she wanted to be away from the threesome at the table. She wanted to be with her patient. "If you all don't mind, I'd like to take my meal upstairs, just in case Jake wakes up."

Oliver and Bob both rose when she did, and they remained standing until she had taken her plate of food and her envelope of cash and left the room. She walked up the stairs and tucked the envelope under her arm to free up a hand for unlocking the door. Then she opened it and went inside.

Her patient was facedown on the floor, dragging himself slowly, painstakingly toward the door.

He heard the woman, the angel, say, "Oh, no!" And she sounded genuinely alarmed. Then she ran into the room, closing the door behind her, depositing whatever she was carrying on the bedside stand. He couldn't really see much above her hips. It was too much work to hold his head up that high. Didn't matter, because in an instant she came to him, knelt beside him and gripped his upper arm. "Let me help you. Come on now, you need to get back into bed."

Her voice was soft, and he loved the feel of it brushing his senses, especially when she was this close and her breath touched his face. It would be easy to do whatever she told him. But despite his instant infatuation with her, he had to consider the possibility that she might be working for them.

"No," he managed.

He tried to keep crawling, but he was weak. His head fell forward, forehead resting on the floor, breath rushing out of him in exhaustion or disappointment or both.

"It's all right," she said, her breath soft on his face

again. "Come on. Let me help you. Please let me help you."

This time when she attempted to roll him onto his back, he let her. He lay there for a long moment, staring up at her. She was on her knees, bending over him, staring at him, and her eyes seemed to get kind of stuck whenever they met his. It seemed an effort for her to tug them free.

She gripped his shoulders and pulled him into a sitting position. It wasn't easy, because he wore pale blue pajamas made of silk, and her hands kept slipping on the fabric. But she got him upright eventually. His head hung forward for a moment, and he could see that she was kneeling, straddling his legs, her hands still on his shoulders. So close... He could smell her, and she smelled good. Really good. He couldn't remember being this intimately close to a woman who smelled as good as she did.

He lifted his head slowly, tried to meet her eyes with his unfocused, unsteady ones. So close... The idea of kissing her crossed his mind. Stupid idea, of course. Utterly impractical, given that there were far more urgent matters that needed attention. He had to get through to her.

But her eyes slid over his face, lingered on his lips, and he thought maybe she was thinking about kissing him, too.

He closed his eyes, because it was the only way he could force himself to stop looking at her mouth and thinking about kisses. He concentrated every neuron in his brain on making his mouth form coherent words. "Not…what…you think."

"I know you're not at your best right now, Handsome," she said softly. "Believe me, I've seen worse. Don't be embarrassed. Come on, let's slide you closer to the bed."

She stood and walked around behind him, then bent low to hook her arms under his. He pushed with his legs, and she tugged him around, then backward, sliding him across the floor, ever closer to the bed. He was sweating with the effort by the time they stopped.

She came around in front of him again, kneeling to put her face level with his. His back was propped against the side of the bed now. "Rest a minute," she told him. "I'll probably have to get Bob to help get you into the—"

"No!" His objection was so vehement that it came out far more loudly than he'd intended. It was clear that it shocked her. "Bob…liar."

She blinked three times, frowning at him. "Your cousin Bob is a liar?" she asked, watching his face closely.

"No…cousin," he managed, panting, forcing out each word with supreme effort.

"He's not your cousin," she interpreted slowly, as if he were speaking some foreign language. "I see."

But she didn't. She couldn't possibly. He had to make her understand.

"Kidnap," he said.

Why she didn't react in shock or horror to that

single word, Zach couldn't begin to guess. Instead she nodded, and her face seemed to fill with pity for him. "You poor man," she whispered, pressing a soft palm to his cheek. "I know. I know, I understand. These people are strangers to you. They came in and they kidnapped you, took you against your will from the only life you knew. And now they're calling you by a name you don't recognize, trying to make you remember things you're certain never happened. And all you want to do is escape here, get your old life back."

She knew? God, she *knew?*

He felt his eyes dampen as he struggled to hold her gaze. He'd so hoped she was not a part of this.

"You see?" she asked him gently. "I *do* understand. And I promise you, I'm going to help you remember these people. They're your family, Jake, and they love you."

"No..."

"Yes, Jake, yes, it's true. But I know you don't believe it now. I'm going to help you to find the truth. You have to help me do that, all right? You have to help me and we'll find the truth together."

God, it was worse than he'd thought. She wasn't a part of the plot, but she was believing the lies these kidnappers had been telling her. That he was family, that he'd lost his memory. God, it was ludicrous.

"Will you help me, Handsome?"

He tried to quell his disappointment. At least she

wasn't one of the criminals. He could still get through to her. He nodded.

"Now let me help you back into bed." She hooked her arms beneath his shoulders, from in front of him this time, and he bent his knees, planted his feet and pushed upward as she pulled. But when he got upright, he fell backward, and with her arms captive beneath his, she fell with him, landing on top of him on the bed.

Time seemed to pause as she lay there, her eyes staring into his, her body pressed tightly against him. One would never know by the feelings surging through him right then that he had been drugged and starved to the point of madness. He didn't feel weak at that moment, or sick or exhausted. He felt strong.

She was beautiful. Soft and small. And she exuded a magnetic pull on his senses that shook awake a part of him he hadn't even known existed. Oh, he'd been with women. Very, very few women. But he'd never felt a pull this powerful with any of them.

She licked her lips and he felt his blood turned to molten lava.

Finally, she seemed to shake herself, then got off him. Bending to lift his legs onto the bed, she helped him straighten out, then propped him up with a pillow. But she avoided his eyes, he noted. And her cheeks were flushed and her breathing quick and shallow.

"There. Now, since you seem to be conscious, would you like to try some food? I've asked them to bring you up some soup later on, but it's not ready yet. Besides, if you can make it halfway across the room, I think you might be able to handle solid food.'' She smiled. ''How about trying some of mine to tide you over?''

He turned his head, not wanting to look away from her. But his body's reaction to the mention of food was almost as powerful as his libido's reaction to her body passing against his. He eyed the plate of food she had left on the bedside stand, and his stomach growled. ''Yours?'' he asked, glad to have the power to speak even one word.

''Yes, it's mine.'' She reached for the plate, and her gaze strayed to the chair lying on its side on the floor, then the water pitcher, which lay toppled in a puddle that soaked into the carpet. She set the plate down again, righted the chair, then picked up the pitcher and glass and carried them into the bathroom attached to his bedroom.

He could see her through the open door. She ran fresh water into the pitcher, rinsing it well first, probably in case any carpet dust had got into it. She repeated the rinsing and filling process with the glass, then took a sip.

''Mmm, this is sweet and cold. Spring fed, I'll bet. No chlorine or fluoride added.'' She carried it back into the bedroom, set the pitcher on the nightstand and offered the glass to Zach.

He took the glass, brought it slowly to his lips, but

his hands shook so badly the water sloshed over the sides, and he nearly dropped it.

She quickly covered his hands with hers, steadying them and guiding the glass to his lips. The feeling of her hands on his was as welcome as the feel of the icy cold water rushing down his parched throat. He didn't trust anything these people brought him to eat or drink, suspecting it could be laced with drugs or poison. But this was safe. And God, how he needed it.

He drank slowly, draining the glass. When he was finished, she took the glass from him and placed it on the stand.

"You're doing so much better already," she said. She pulled her plate into her lap, then took her fork and worked a piece of chicken free of the golden brown leg. She offered it to him. "Try this. It smells delicious."

He drew back, shook his head very slightly, unsure. She'd said it was hers, but was it really? Could he be certain it was safe?

"Come on, Handsome. I don't think you'll manage to stay awake much longer, do you? And I really want some sustenance in you before you go to sleep again."

He ought to be in a hospital with intravenous lines running into him, he thought vaguely. Whatever they'd been giving him was turning his brain into oatmeal. He was beginning to doubt his own mind.

"What's wrong? You don't like chicken?"

He lifted a hand, pointed to her.

"You want me to eat first?"

His slow, relieved sigh must have told her she had hit the nail on the head. "Now is that because you're a gentleman, or because you think someone's trying to poison you, hmm?" She popped the chicken into her mouth. "Mmm, delicious. Gee, you know, it tastes oddly familiar." She shrugged and took another bite.

He was reacting in every possible way to watching her eat. The way her lips closed around the food, the way her mouth moved as she chewed, the gentle "mmm" sounds she was made, and his own hunger all mixed together to create a yearning for her and the food that was so intense it was almost frightening.

Gave a whole new meaning to the word *hunger*.

He fought to keep his focus, and struggled to utter a single word. "Drugs."

She frowned as she chewed. "Drugs? Did you say…?" She swallowed the bite and started over. "Are you trying to tell me you think your family has been drugging your food?"

He nodded, then glanced at the water pitcher.

"And the water, too?" she asked. "Is that why you spilled it? God, no wonder they can't get you to eat. And that's why you're so weak, too. Listen, from now on, no one touches your food but me, okay? I promise you, I'll make sure. That way you won't need to be afraid to eat."

He nodded. He trusted her. And he told himself that

was because he had no choice but to trust her. If she was on their side, he was history. But if he didn't eat soon, he wasn't going to make it, anyway.

There was more to it, though, and he knew that. He had a feeling he'd have trusted this particular woman if she told him it was snowing at the Alamo. She picked up another bit of chicken in her small fingers and offered it to him. He took it into his mouth, tasting her fingertips along with it.

They finished the meal together, with the beautiful doctor taking the first bite of everything, from the potatoes and gravy to the biscuit to the vegetables. He ate all he could hold, and then drank more water.

His eyelids were heavy, his body slumping in the bed, and he knew he had to get some sleep soon. The drugs, the escape attempts, the late-night madness were taking their toll. He could barely keep his eyes open.

"As long as you're talking," she said, smiling at him, "think you can tell me what name you prefer I call you?"

He held her eyes, his own struggling to stay focused as he formed the word. "Z-Z-Zach."

"Zach." She frowned. "Hmm. Not your typical cult-commune-generated name, is it?" Then she shrugged. "I'm Maisy," she said softly. "Nobody calls me that, though. Mostly it's M.J. or Dr. Dalton."

Sighing in apparent relief, he let his body relax against the pillows, but then he thought of something he hadn't before.

Maisy reached out to tug his covers over him. He closed his hand around her wrist, and when she looked at his face, he tried to tell her with his eyes just how important his next words would be. "Don't...t-tell...thhh...mmm. Thhhhem.

"Don't tell them?" she repeated.

He nodded, relaxing his head on the pillows.

"Don't tell them what, Zach? Your name? Or that you're eating again?"

Without opening his eyes this time, he muttered, "Nothing. Tell...nothing."

"All right. I'll tell them nothing. You're my patient, Zach. They aren't. If you ask me to keep a confidence, I'm obligated to do it. You can trust me on that."

His head moved, almost a nod but not quite. He trusted her and the Hippocratic oath had nothing to do with it. It was illogical but nothing that had happened to him over the past few days was logical anyway, so it fit right in.

Four

He was sinking into sleep, she realized. She sighed in relief. Progress already, and so soon. It was a shame he didn't recognize his family or remember his past. It was also a shame that he didn't believe he had ever been Jake Smith. God, that he so mistrusted his relatives he thought they might be drugging his food...

But it was normal for a person who'd been forcibly abducted from a cult environment to mistrust his rescuers at first. It took time to undo the programming of a charismatic leader. Mind control was easy, especially if the subject was weak-willed or wanted to believe the things he was being told. Zach, as he called himself, didn't seem to her to be the weak-willed type. So he must have been desperate to believe in whatever rhetoric his cult leader had been preaching.

Funny that he hadn't mentioned the man, the leader. Usually, in cases like this, it was the one thing the patients would go on and on about.

Sighing, she tucked him more thoroughly into bed, ignoring the stirring awareness the man managed to generate in her. She had no business feeling those kinds of things for a patient. She, more than anyone, knew better.

Maisy got to her feet and took the dinner plate and silverware with her back down the stairs.

The others were no longer in the kitchen. She wasn't certain where they'd gone, because she didn't hear a sound. The house felt empty. The table had been cleared and wiped down, the dishes washed. The place was spotless. She looked for a trash bin, someplace to toss the chicken bones from the plate. She knew better than to toss them out the front door to the dog, and not just because he would likely snap her arm off. While she disliked the Smiths' dog intensely, she didn't want to harm it by feeding it splinter-prone chicken bones.

Ahh, there was a blue kitchen-size wastebasket, with a swinging white lid, lined by a clear plastic garbage bag. She dumped the bones inside, then paused. Frowning at the familiar red-and-white-striped container that sat atop the other garbage. It bore the logo of a popular chain of fried chicken restaurants. No wonder the chicken had tasted so familiar to her. She'd had it before. Many times. And the potatoes, gravy and biscuits, too.

Wasn't that the oddest thing? For Agnes to go to so much trouble to make it appear as if she had cooked this meal, to the point of pouring every course out of its takeout foam container into a nice serving dish.

Maybe she couldn't cook and was embarrassed to

admit it. Maisy supposed the ranch wife image was littered with stereotypes, just like everything else. Maybe not all of them cooked huge, delicious, high-calorie meals with ease, after all.

Shrugging, Maisy washed her plate and silverware, stacked them with the others in the drainer and wiped her hands on a small dish towel.

Then she headed back upstairs, still seeing no one. After peeking into Zach's room, she went in search of her own. Bob had told her that her bedroom was next to Zach's. There were only two choices. She tried the door to the left first, and it opened easily, into a room that was dark and dusty. Chunks of plaster hung from the ceiling, revealing the bare lathe boards underneath. Pieces of fallen plaster littered the floor, which was made up of broad, naked boards. The window had been washed, and a set of curtains hung up, but the rest of the room looked as if it hadn't been used in years.

A little shiver slid down Maisy's spine, but she shook it off. It wasn't all that unusual for an old farmhouse like this to have an unused room or two. Of course, she would have expected the Smiths to use the room for storage. It was just creepy to see it so empty and ramshackle. Somehow it felt wrong. Like so many other things around here.

She backed out of the room, closing the door, and turned down the hallway to the room on the right, half afraid of what she might find there. But when she opened the door, she sighed in relief. The room had been made ready for her. There was fresh yellow paint on the walls and what looked and smelled like new beige carpet on the floor. A single, four-poster bed awaited her, with brand-new, crisp bedding, a bright yellow sunflower print on a white background. There was a small dresser and an alarm clock beside the bed. No TV. No artwork on the walls. There was one window, dressed in curtains that matched the bedspread.

She saw her overnight bag on the bed and noted the door at one end of the room. Opening it, she saw a familiar bathroom, with another door on its opposite wall that led into Zach's room. That was good. Perfect, in fact.

She opened both bathroom doors, giving her a clear line of sight and sound to Zach. Then she realized that she was alone, her work was done, her patient asleep and his demanding family members conveniently absent. Finally, she could sit down and relax.

She unzipped her overnight bag and dug inside for the newspaper. She was going to put her feet up, and read quietly for a little while.

But the newspaper wasn't there. Either she'd never put it into her bag in the first place—something she clearly remembered doing—or someone had taken it.

But who? And perhaps more importantly, why?

It was late. She was tired, and possibly not thinking quite as clearly as she should. Always a planner, a strategist, a careful, deliberate thinker, Maisy decided to take a few moments to write the orders for the hospital lab, and then to get to bed and think about all of this some more. In the morning she would get some answers.

In the morning Maisy woke to the smell of brewing coffee. It tickled her senses to life, and she rolled over in bed, glanced at the clock. Seven a.m. The sun was pouring in through the bedroom window. It would be a good day. If she made as much progress with Jake—with Zach—today, as she had in a single night, there might be a major breakthrough. She so wanted him to be able to communicate with her in more than just one- or two-word sentences. She so wanted to reach him.

Still, she was leaning toward taking him out of here. If he didn't trust his family, this probably wasn't the environment most conducive to his recovery. But she would make that decision today.

She rolled out of bed and walked into the bathroom. The door into Zach's room was closed. It hadn't been closed when she'd gone to bed last night. She turned the knob and found it locked from the other side.

What the hell?

Alarmed, she hurried back through her own bedroom, out into the hallway. Zach's door was locked from there, too—from the outside. She quickly undid the bolt and went to check on her patient.

Zach lay in the bed, sound asleep. His arms were

once again bound to the bed frame, his face damp with sweat.

Fury rose up in her chest like a fireball, and she hurried to the bedside, yanking the knots free and throwing the ropes angrily to the floor. His forearms were crisscrossed with angry red lines, as if he'd struggled against the bindings. She rubbed them to get the circulation going, and tried to quell her rage. She was going to give someone hell for this.

"Zach. Hey, wake up, come on." She forced her voice to sound calm, reassuring, so as not to alarm him.

He didn't move, didn't open his eyes or respond in any way. She could hear him breathing, but slowly. Maisy closed her hand around his wrist, her fingers pressing gently. His pulse was slow, but steady. She patted his face with her palm. "Come on, wake up now."

Nothing.

With her jaw clenched, Maisy surged out of the bedroom and down the stairs, through the house into the kitchen. Bob was standing by the coffeepot, filling two mugs, and he looked up, smiling way too warmly and holding one out to her.

"I heard you up moving around," he said. "Coffee?"

"Bob, what the hell happened last night?"

He frowned at her, setting her cup on the table, then adding creamer to his own. "With Jake, you mean?"

"Yes, with Jake. I told you I didn't want him restrained, and yet I get up this morning to find him locked in his room and tied to the bed again."

Bob lowered his eyes, shaking his head slowly. "I really was surprised you didn't wake up, Dr. Dalton, what with all the commotion." He sighed, a deep, heavy sigh. "Sit down and drink your coffee while I explain."

She sat down, certain no explanation was going to be good enough.

"When I went upstairs to look in on Jake last night, he wasn't in his bed. I saw the bathroom door open, so I went in there. He was heading into your room, and he had a knife. I don't know where he managed to get it from, but let me tell you, it was lucky I came in when I did. I don't know what he might have done."

He could have sprouted horns and shocked her less. She sat there, speechless, shaking her head in disbelief.

"I pulled him back into his room and took the knife away. I only locked the doors and restrained him because I feared for your safety. He's not himself, Dr. Dalton."

She frowned, studying him with narrow eyes. "I'm a *very* light sleeper, Bob. I don't know how all that could have happened without my waking up."

He shook his head. "He didn't fight me much. Course, he isn't very strong right now, and maybe he knew it would be useless. Or maybe he didn't want you to know what he was up to. I don't know."

"So all this happened without any noise at all?" she asked.

"Hardly any. He was standing over your bed with a knife. I took the knife away, grabbed his arm and pulled, and he came right along. I put him to bed. He didn't even fight me a bit when I tied him down. I doubt we made much noise at all." He lowered his eyes, as if his big heart were breaking.

"Do you think maybe you ought to give him something? You know, keep him sedated? Or would that slow down his progress in getting his memory back?"

She shook her head. "Certain drugs might actually help stimulate his memory, but I'm not about to give him anything until I know what's already in his bloodstream." Then she frowned, looking up at Bob. "You haven't been giving him anything, have you?"

"Hell, no. We're not doctors, we're just simple ranchers."

She studied his face for a long moment. Could he be lying? But what reason would he have to lie to her? "I couldn't wake him up this morning, Bob. I don't know what could put him into the state he's in right now, besides drugs. And I can't help him if you're not honest with me."

Bob shook his head. "We haven't given him anything. Honest."

"Maybe I should talk to Agnes and Oliver," she

said, glancing around the kitchen, wondering for the first time why they hadn't yet put in an appearance.

"They've gone."

"Already?"

Bob smiled, the previous subject apparently already forgotten. "My dad likes to get an early start on long trips."

"But—but they didn't take the blood, or the orders I wrote—"

"Sure they did," he told her. "I saw the note on your nightstand when I was up there with Jake last night. I brought it down for them then. Say, did you want to call that hospital lab, let 'em know the blood sample is on the way? Come to think of it, once they run those tests for you, you'll know exactly what kind of drugs are in my cousin's bloodstream—or whether there are any at all."

He was right; she would. And while she'd told Bob she didn't know of any non-drug-related reasons Zach would be so deeply unconscious, it wasn't quite true. Some mental conditions could cause that kind of state, as could certain chemical imbalances. She sipped her coffee, wondering why she was so inclined to let the rantings of a mental patient put doubts in her mind about his well-meaning family members.

"I really feel very strongly that Jake should be in a hospital, Bob."

"I know, but my parents are dead set against it," he said. "Besides, given the state of mind he's in, you couldn't treat him without the consent of a relative, could you?''

"I could if I had to. But it would take some time. But you could give consent, Bob. You're a relative.''

Bob shook his head firmly. "I won't go against my parents' wishes in this, much less go behind their backs.''

"Even if it means saving your cousin from this hell he's in right now?''

Bob sighed. "Look, Mom and Dad will call in tonight. They always call every night while they're away. I'll explain the situation and get my mother's okay. Or at least tell her that we have to go ahead with or without it.''

Maisy lifted her brows. "You'd do that?''

He pursed his lips. "To save Jake, yeah. Mom won't like it, but if I have to, I will. I just can't go behind her back. I have to tell her the truth. You give me time to do that, and I promise you, I'll be happy to sign a consent form.''

Maisy nodded slowly. It wasn't perfect, but it might be the best she was going to achieve right now. It would take at least a day, possibly longer, to get Zach ruled incapable of making decisions on his own and to convince a judge to order him hospitalized. Longer, with the family fighting it. Giving Bob today, keeping him on her side, might be the best way to get Zach the help he needed.

"Meantime," Bob added, "why don't we just see

how today goes, what the blood tests show, and then decide the rest tonight, when my parents call in?''

Sighing, she nodded. ''I've already decided, Bob. I'll give you today to get used to the idea and break it to your parents, but I'm going to hold you to your promise. I want him in a hospital tonight.''

She got up from the table and walked to the old-fashioned black wall-mounted telephone to call the hospital lab. The phone had a rotary dial. She went through the operator, since she didn't know the number by heart and didn't see a telephone book anywhere around.

Within a few minutes, the call was placed.

''Austin Memorial Hospital, Hematology Lab. Can I help you?''

''This is Dr. M. J. Dalton,'' she said, using her crisp, professional voice. ''I'm sending a blood sample over there this morning. A couple by the name of Smith will be dropping it off for me along with my written instructions. I'm going to need a complete toxicology screen and I need it as fast as possible. How soon can you do that for me?''

''If we have the sample this morning, we can probably have some preliminary results before day's end, Dr. Dalton. Is that soon enough?''

''It'll have to be. Can you make a note to have someone phone me as soon as you have anything?''

''Sure thing. The number?''

She read the number from the telephone dial, then gave her cell-phone number as well, before remembering that there was no reception out here in the middle of nowhere. "You'll be more likely to reach me at the first number than the second," she told them.

"And the name of the patient?"

"Za— That is, Jake Smith."

"Insurance?"

Maisy turned to Bob. "Insurance?"

He shook his head. Maisy spoke into the mouthpiece. "No insurance. Just bill it to me. All my information is on file with the hospital."

She heard clicking keys, then, "Yes, here you are. All right, Dr. Dalton, we're all set on this end. I'll probably be off duty by the time the results come in, but I'm leaving a note for the next shift to be sure they know to call you the minute they have anything to report."

"Thanks. I appreciate it."

"No problem. You have a nice day, Dr. Dalton."

"You, too." Maisy hung up the phone. She didn't like this. She didn't like it at all.

"Breakfast?" Bob asked.

She pursed her lips, remembering her patient's insistence that his food was being drugged. Normally she wouldn't have given the claim a second thought, but now, given his condition this morning, she had to wonder if his relatives were overstepping in their efforts to help him.

"No, I'll have something later," she said finally.

He nodded. "You enjoy your coffee, then. Me, I've

got to do some chores this morning. Horses and cattle need tending.''

''Go ahead, I can handle things here.''

''Are you sure? Suppose Jake wakes up and gets violent again?''

He wouldn't. She knew he wouldn't. And that was a completely unscientific, nonobjective notion. Why she even allowed it to float through her mind was beyond her. She was doubting the word of an apparently sane, normal man in favor of that of an obviously disturbed patient.

A patient to whom she felt an undeniable attraction, though she hated like hell to admit that. She'd need to be careful not to allow that unprofessional feeling to cloud her judgment. Though she was afraid she was already letting it do just that, and that was yet another reason to get Zach into a hospital bed. It was a far less intimate setting.

''I'll tranquilize him if it becomes absolutely necessary,'' she said. ''But not unless it does, and I really don't think it will.''

Bob nodded. ''I'll be within earshot. Worse comes to worse, you can shout out the window and I'll come running.''

''Thanks. That's reassuring.''

It wasn't. But it probably should have been.

Bob left the house. The second he did, Maisy jumped up from the table and poured her coffee down the drain. Then she emptied the pot, rinsed it thoroughly and brewed a fresh one. While it was dripping, she raided the fridge, located eggs, bread, butter. She fixed a breakfast for two: eggs and toast for her, a protein shake of raw eggs, milk and some sugar for her patient, who probably wouldn't be up to chewing this morning.

Then she carefully washed, dried and put away every dish and pan she had used, being very careful to put them in exactly the same places, the same positions as they had been when she'd found them.

It was as she was hanging the dish towel on the rack, attempting to get it to hang just the way it had been before, that she stopped and took a look at herself. God, she was acting as paranoid as poor, deluded Zach up there.

She swallowed hard, questioning her judgment.

And then she decided it was better to err on the side of caution.

Bob left the house. On the way out, he disconnected the telephone line, not from the wall jack inside the house, but from the box on the outside. Easy enough to reconnect, should he need it. But not for her. She wouldn't even know where the box was.

Then he went out to tend to the four horses and ten cows Agnes had insisted were necessary "for authenticity." He took the rifle with him. The one with the long-range scope.

Five

The angel was back. He felt her hovering nearby, could almost hear the soft flutter of her wings beating the air. The soft glow of her aura penetrated his eyelids. He felt her warmth, right through the covers.

Last night, when Bob had come and the nightly torture had begun again, Zach had wondered where his angel had gone, whether she had abandoned him, whether she had just been a dream all along.

She was back now, or maybe she had never left. He felt her, sensed her, smelled her, saw her without opening his eyes. But was she an angel, after all? If she had been here the whole time, had she known what was going on and just ignored it? Let it happen?

He tried to think back, but the damned drugs were making his mind hazy and unreliable. He hadn't seen her last night. Or he didn't think he had. And he remembered noticing how quiet Bob had been about everything. Usually, once he had Zach tied to the bed, with the blinding light in his eyes and the drugs coursing through his veins, he got impatient and the endless, senseless questions came out louder and more demanding as he went along.

Agnes never got loud when it was her turn. Her

voice was a drone that was almost hypnotic. Oliver never participated. He'd watched once, but left halfway through the session. Probably didn't have the stomach for it.

What about the angel?

Zach wanted to believe she had no part in this madness, whatever the hell it was. His mind was so clouded by drugs that it was difficult for him to make much sense of anything, he realized that. But he was starting to understand that even at his best, he wouldn't have been able to make much sense of this.

He opened his eyes. Maisy had brought a plate of food and a glass containing some sort of shake, with a straw sticking out the top of it. She set them both on the bedside stand, then took his water pitcher and glass into the bathroom, emptied them, rinsed them out, and refilled them with fresh, cold water.

He sighed in relief. Maybe she was starting to understand that he wasn't the crazy one in this house.

When she came back and put the pitcher down, she sat not in the chair, but on the edge of his mattress. It surprised him when she leaned over, stroked his hair away from his face as she searched his eyes.

"Glad to see you awake," she said, her voice soft, barely above a whisper. "I don't know exactly what happened last night, Zach, but I'm sorry about it. When I got up this morning and found you tied to the bed again—" She broke off there, her jaw clenched so tight it made her face tremble. "It won't happen again. I promise you that. If I have to sleep in here to see to it, I will.''

He blinked slowly, the only way he felt able to answer her right now.

''I just don't understand why things seem to have worsened for you, Zach. You were doing so much better last night. Talking, even.''

He licked his lips, focused every bit of energy he had on speaking, just a word. Just a single word. ''D-d-drrrr...ugs.''

She sat there, staring at him. He shifted his gaze down to his right arm, then back to her, then to the arm again. Frowning hard, she looked down at his arm, her hands moving over it, thumb stroking the bend in his elbow, head lowering even closer as she squinted. She saw it. He knew she saw it when her hand went still and her eyes widened.

''Oh my God.'' It was a whisper. A mere whisper.

''Book,'' he managed to utter. And again he used his eyes to guide her. She followed his gaze to the book of nursery rhymes that sat on the nightstand. And he knew that she would know it hadn't been there the night before.

She picked the book up, thumbed through it. With her voice still just a whisper, she said, ''Zach, are you telling me that they came in here last night, injected you with something, tied you to the bed and then read to you from this book?''

He nodded as forcefully as he could. They'd done a lot more than that, but she got the general idea.

She searched his eyes, his face. He thought she looked scared. She said, "I want you to tell me the truth now, Zach. Did you ever get out of bed last night? Did you pick up a knife and come into my room with it?"

He shook his head from side to side. When she looked away, he reached up and touched her cheek, so that she faced him again in surprise. "Never... h-h-hurt...you." He took a breath, forced the words to come, though it was so much effort he was breaking out in a sweat. "My...on...ly...hope."

Why was it so easy for her to believe him? The mark in his arm could have just as easily been made four days earlier, before he'd been rescued from the compound. But there was no questioning the fact that she'd found him bound to the bed, locked in the room this morning. And there was no question that the book of nursery rhymes hadn't been out when she'd left him last night.

"I am going to get you out of here," she promised him. "Today." She could no longer risk that what he was telling her might be true, even if it was far-fetched and barely likely. In a hospital, there wouldn't be a question. And she couldn't treat the man when she was doubting herself at every turn. God, why did she believe him?

He shook his head. "Your...car."

"What about my car?" she asked.

He glanced toward the window, and she looked

where he did. Her car was in plain sight of his bedroom window.

"B-Bob…"

"Bob what?"

Zach shook his head slowly, from side to side.

Was he trying to tell her that Bob had tampered with her car? Zach certainly had a bird's-eye view of her vehicle from here, but still.

She hurried through the bathroom into her room, retrieved her keys from her bag and then returned to Zach's side. "I'll just be a second. Bob's out seeing to the livestock, and the others are away." She hated to leave him, knowing it made no sense to feel that way. Then she went to the window, flipped the lock and opened it. It didn't open easily. In fact it acted as if it hadn't been opened in a long, long time. "There. If he comes near you, make some noise. All right?"

He nodded once. "Don't…"

He couldn't seem to finish, but she leaned over him. "Don't what?"

He gripped her hand, prying her keys from it. Then he held them, mimicking the motions of inserting them into the switch, turning them to start the car. She was getting more frightened by the minute. "Don't start the engine?"

He sighed, nodding hard.

"All right," she said. "I won't. But I have to at least take a look."

"Careful," he warned.

Maisy nodded, believing him right to her core. Someone had done something to her car. His mind might not be functioning properly right now, but his eyes were sincere and intense. Maybe his imagination had enhanced what he'd seen. But there was no doubt in her mind that he believed what he was telling her.

She had to make a supreme effort to tug her gaze from his, but once she did, she turned and ran out of the room and down the stairs. As she neared the bottom, though, she forced herself to slow her pace. There was no sense in alarming Bob. There was probably no sense in letting herself become this agitated over the word of a patient who was in such a confused state of mind. He could have imagined, or even dreamed, everything he'd told her this morning.

Right. But he didn't imagine those ropes around his arms, or that needle prick in his skin. And I didn't imagine the look in his eyes. He was afraid for me, really, truly afraid.

She fought to stop shaking, and stepped into the living room, looking around for Bob, but seeing no one. Next, she checked the kitchen. There were other rooms on the ground floor of the house, rooms she had never been in, but she decided not to bother with them. Not now. Now all she wanted to do was get to her car and assure herself that it hadn't been tampered with.

She opened the screen door, and it creaked in protest. Then she stepped out onto the porch, glanced left and right, still seeing no one. Her car was in the driveway, just as she'd left it. Stepping down the porch steps, careful to miss the broken ones, she walked quickly to her car, her keys in hand.

The dog scrambled out from under the porch like lightning, lunging at her, jaws snapping as it barked, saliva flying in a hundred directions. Maisy exploded into motion, racing for the car. The dog launched itself into the air, its jaws closing powerfully on her upper arm, tearing flesh, sending her to her knees with the force of its weight. She reacted instinctively, twisting around and punching the slathering snout as hard as she could with her free hand. The dog released its hold and Maisy scrambled away like a crab across the dirt, to the car.

The beast was at the far end of its chain now, snapping at air six inches short of her face. It couldn't quite reach her, but it was close enough that she could smell its breath. Her keys, on the other hand, were in the dust under its paws. She couldn't get back to the house, and she couldn't leave. Clutching her torn upper arm with her hand to keep the blood from flowing too fast, her eyes never leaving the dog, she managed to slide her back up the side of the car until she was standing. She reached behind her, fumbled with the car door and opened it.

"You goin' somewhere, Dr. Dalton?"

Maisy spun around, facing Bob. He stood on the passenger side of the car looking at her over the top. "I just…wanted something from my car."

He frowned at her. "Ah, hell, that dog nipped you,

didn't he? Rufus, damn you, go lie down!'' he shouted.

The dog stopped barking and cowered a little.

''Git!''

The animal slunk back to its place of ambush underneath the porch. ''You'd best come on inside and let me see to that wound for you. Looks nasty.''

She kept the pressure on it, felt the blood oozing.

''Damn dog. You know we only have him so he can keep the wolves and coyotes away from the livestock.'' Bob was coming around the car now, looking worriedly at her arm.

''How does he do that, chained up to the porch?''

''Oh, we set him loose at night,'' he said, glancing at the ground where her keys were lying. ''He patrols the place as well as a trained watchman could do. He's our own little soldier.'' Bending down, Bob scooped up her keys, dropped them into his pocket. ''Next time you need something, Dr. Dalton, you just say so. I'll be happy to get you anything you want.''

He took her elbow gently and walked close beside her back into the house. She never heard another peep from the dog. They went up the porch steps, and through the creaking screen door. Bob nudged her into a chair at the kitchen table, then walked into the room off the left side of the kitchen. In most homes, she would have guessed that to be the dining room. Here, she couldn't be sure of anything. She craned her neck to watch his progress. He went through another door at the far end.

She'd never dressed this morning. She was still wearing a T-shirt nightie and a knee-length cotton robe the sleeve of which was now torn and bloody. She peeled the robe off carefully, wincing as she did, then went to the sink, cranked on the taps and thrust her arm under the rushing water. It hurt like hell.

As the blood washed down the drain, she saw that the damage wasn't as bad as it felt. There were two large tears where the animal's incisors had pierced her flesh and then pulled. They could have taken a couple of stitches each, but would heal as well with a bandage job.

Bob reappeared with his hands full of medical supplies—antibacterial soap, antibiotic ointment, gauze and tape. "He's had all his shots. You needn't worry about rabies or anything like that," he said.

She nodded and shut the water off.

"Sit down now and let me patch you up."

"I'll do it myself." She tugged a dish towel from the rack, laid it on the table and placed all the items atop it. "And I'd just as soon take my car keys as well," she said.

"Oh. Right. I forgot. Sorry about that." He dipped in his pocket for the keys and added them to her little pile with a sheepish shrug.

She gathered the ends of the towel, picking up all the items with it. "Bob, I don't want to be rude here, but if you want me to stay on your cousin's case for so much as another hour, that dog has to go. I'm afraid I have to insist. If you can't move him, I have to leave right now."

"But the wolves—"

"That beast is more dangerous than any wolf." She pursed her lips. "If you have to have him around, can't you put him out in the barn or something until I leave?" She almost added that it would only be for today, since she had no intention of letting Zach remain here another night. He needed a hospital. But something, some bit of Zach's paranoia, which must be a new, contagious strain, made her keep that to herself.

Bob tipped his head to one side. "Well, I can't say as I blame you for being upset with Rufus. My mother will likely skin me alive for letting you get hurt. I'll move the dog. You won't have to see him again, I promise."

She was a little surprised that he would cooperate so easily. Especially if Zach's wild theories were true and Bob was some kind of criminal, holding Zach, and Maisy as well, prisoner in this place. "Really?"

"Well, of course. Geez, you think I want you to leave?" He reached out, gently pushing a strand of hair off her forehead. "You're our only hope of getting our Jake back, Dr. Dalton. I'll do whatever it takes to keep you on this case." Then he shrugged. "Besides, I kind of like having you around."

Was he flirting with her? Oh, God, that was all she needed.

"Now if there's anything else you need, anything at all, you just let me know. Okay?"

Not quite able to formulate a verbal reply, she nodded, then took her bundle and hurried up the stairs.

Zach managed to sit up in the bed long enough to watch the woman when she went outside, and he saw the dog lunge, saw it bite, and felt more helpless than he ever had in his entire life. Every muscle in his body tensed, even knowing he was too far away and too goddamn weak to be of any help to her.

She got away, but it could have been disastrous. He could have sat there, helpless, and watched the dog rip her to pieces. He *hated* that he was up here, too weak and foggy-brained to be of any assistance at all.

Dammit.

He'd never been the macho, physical, heroic type. He was an economics professor, for God's sake. But he liked to think he would have put himself between the woman and that dog, had he been able to.

Time passed like chilled molasses as he waited for her return. Finally he heard her steps in the hall, and the door opened and she came inside.

He swept his gaze over her, noting that the robe she'd worn before was stained in scarlet and draped over her wounded arm. She clutched a bundled-up dish towel in that hand, too, while her other hand was pressed to her upper arm.

He met her eyes, searched them.

"It's okay, it's superficial." She closed the door with her hip, came to the bed and dropped the towel on the nightstand.

As it fell open, he saw the items inside—gauze, ointment, tape and alcohol. She got up on the edge of the bed beside him, reached for the rubbing alcohol first. She twisted off the cap, soaked a gauze pad in the stuff, then bit her lip.

He touched her hand, and when she met his eyes, he shook his head. "Don't."

"That dog might be carrying anything," she said. "I know it's gonna hurt like hell, but I have to." Then she gave him a shaky smile. "Trust me, I'm a doctor."

He returned her smile, offered his hand. She closed hers around it. "Thanks. I'm gonna need that."

He pursed his lips, nodded. Then he could only sit there, unable to help her while she pressed the alcohol-soaked gauze to the wound, her teeth bared, her eyes watering, her head tipped back. Her hand tightened around his, her nails biting deeply into his flesh. He sat up higher in the bed, leaned close to the wounded left arm and blew gently, repeatedly, on the wound.

She lowered her head slowly, her breaths coming fast. "Thanks," she said in a strained whisper. "God, that hurts."

Swallowing hard, she let go of his hand. Then she smeared a lot of the ointment onto a gauze pad, laid it across the puncture wounds and started tearing off strips of adhesive tape to hold it on. By the time she'd finished, she had made a decent, if one-handed, job of patching herself up.

Then she glanced at him. "I never got much of a chance to check out my car. Bob made a point of mentioning that the beast out there is unfettered at night. Rufus apparently has run of the place."

Zach shook his head slowly. "Trapped."

"That's what I thought at first, too. But when I told Bob to take the dog to the barn and keep him away from me, he didn't even argue. Said he'd do whatever I wanted. And I think he was being straight with me, Zach."

He was shaking his head.

"I know. I know you don't trust him. And I still plan to get you out of here and into a hospital before the day is out."

"He...won't...allow..."

She held up a hand. "You don't think he's going to let us leave. I know, Zach, but I think he will. And I'm taking precautions, just in case. The next time he leaves the house, I'm going to call some friends of mine, let them know what's going on, just in case. If we don't show up, they'll send some help out here."

He nodded, but deep down he doubted she was going to get any such opportunity. Bob wasn't an idiot. If he was, Zach would have been out of here before Maisy ever arrived.

"Zach, you have to give them the benefit of the doubt. Just because I'm taking precautions doesn't mean that you might not be wrong about all of this. There's every chance, every likelihood in fact, that they are acting with the best of intentions, that they really are your family and that they truly love you.''

"Strangers," he said. He seemed to be regaining the ability to put his thoughts into words, though slowly. It still took effort, but the resulting sounds were far more comprehensible to his ears than they had been before. ''Not family.''

She lowered her head, nodding slowly.

He clasped her uninjured arm, so she looked up fast. "Really," he said. Then he pointed at himself. "Zach Ingram."

She frowned at him, making her brown eyes appear serious and even deeper than before. "Ingram?"

He nodded.

"Not Jake Smith?"

Swallowing hard, he focused, concentrated and spoke as slowly and clearly as he could. "Jake Ingram...is...my...brother."

He saw her eyes widen. "You have a brother named Jake? But not Smith. Ingram?"

He nodded.

"Why would they keep insisting that your name is Jake?" she asked.

"Look...alike." He sighed. God, it was such an effort just to carry on this caveman-level conversation.

"He's your twin?"

He shook his head and repeated, "Look alike."

"Okay, okay, so you and your brother look alike. These people keep calling you Jake because they think you're him. But Zach, that doesn't make any sense. If Jake is the one who's actually their nephew, Bob's cousin, then they'd still be your relatives. Not strangers." She frowned hard. "God, that name sounds familiar to me. Jake Ingram. Where have I heard it before?"

"World...Bank..." Zach stopped there, not bothering to finish. He could see in her eyes the moment realization dawned.

She looked at him squarely and said, "Oh my God. You're really not making any of this up, are you?"

"No."

"No. No, of course you're not. Hell, Zach, I think I may be in over my head here."

He closed his eyes. "Me, too."

He heard the screen door slam, then footsteps plodding around downstairs. Bob was back, and he would no doubt be coming up here to check on him soon.

"Have to...pretend," he told her, hoping to God she would understand what he meant.

She shot him a narrow-eyed look. "You're right. We can't let Bob—or the other two should they show up again—know that we're on to them. We have to play along with this scheme of theirs, whatever it is. Just let them think I'm buying into it." She licked her lips. "And I have an idea about the drugs, too. I just need a little time."

He looked past her, at the food she'd brought up

here and never eaten. A plate with scrambled eggs and toast sat on the nightstand, untouched. He'd managed to down the shake she'd mixed up for him, despite his weakness and shaking hands. "Maisy," he said.

She emerged from her state of intense concentration and met his eyes. Her eyes were something to see, he thought. Intelligent, nearly always in motion, but when they went still they were luminous and mesmerizing...and a little bit sad.

"Eat," he told her.

She smiled at him. "Eat. Right, at a time like this?"

He nodded.

She glanced at the plate of cold food, made a face. "I'll eat half if you'll eat half."

"Deal," he said.

"Whatever they gave you, it's wearing off."

He nodded. "Hope so."

"Me, too."

He glanced at her arm. "Sorry."

"What, this?" she asked, shrugging her shoulder. "This is nothing for you to be sorry about. That mongrel, on the other hand, is in deep trouble. And I'm not too thrilled with the dog right now, either."

He got the joke, laughed softly. "Like you," he told her when his smile faded but their eyes still held.

"I'm glad. I like you, too, Zach."

Six

Maisy needed a shower, and she still hadn't dressed. Now that she thought about it, she imagined poor Zach would kill for a bath and a change of clothes, too, by now. She didn't think his loving "family" had been taking very good care of his physical needs. That should have been apparent to her sooner.

She wasn't going to leave her patient alone long enough to take a shower while Bob was in the house, though. She would just have to wait.

On the pretense of refilling her coffee cup, she wandered downstairs, to get a handle on Bob's whereabouts. She found him in the living room, reading what looked like her newspaper. He folded it quickly when she came down the stairs, knocked a sofa pillow on top of it so she couldn't read the headlines.

Of course she knew now what it was he didn't want her to see. She remembered catching a glimpse of the headline yesterday as she'd added the newspaper to her overnight bag for the trip out here. Jake Ingram had been hired to help solve the World Bank heist. The same Jake Ingram these people thought they had drugged into a stupor in their upstairs bedroom, if Zach's theory was correct. She hoped that Bob didn't have ready access to any more recent news reports around here, and guessed he probably didn't. If there had been an issue of today's paper, Bob wouldn't have been desperate to read her old issue. Hell, Agnes and Oliver had probably forbidden television, radio or newspapers in the house in an effort to keep her from catching on. And that was good. It was going to work to her and Zach's benefit for the Smiths not to know they had the wrong Ingram brother—at least not right away. They would find out the truth if and when Maisy decided to let them. Not one minute sooner.

"Hello, Dr. Dalton," Bob said, getting to his feet and putting on a friendly smile. "You need a break? I can sit with him for a while if you—"

"No, he's sound asleep. I just came down to get some more of that coffee."

He nodded, falling into step beside her and walking her into the kitchen. "I can't tell you how sorry I am about your arm."

"It'll heal," she said. "You know, I have to take part of the blame. I knew the dog was out there, I just let it slip my mind. I should have been more careful."

"I've moved him farther from the house," he said. "Out by the barn, just as you asked."

"I appreciate that."

"How's it going with Jake?"

She sighed, shaking her head slowly, sinking into a kitchen chair. "I'm afraid whatever they gave him at that compound must have been pretty powerful. He's still out of touch with reality."

"I was afraid of that." Bob took her empty mug to the coffeepot, filled it and brought it back to her before sitting down across from her. "Do you think he'll ever get his memory back?"

"Oh, yes. I have no doubt about that."

Bob's head came up, his eyes sharp. "Why, has he remembered something already?"

A little shiver went up her spine. Clearly, part of this plot involved Jake Ingram's memory. But why?

"Not yet," she said, choosing her words with care. "But I can tell the defenses he's built up are falling away, layer by layer. I'll be able to get through to him in time."

"I don't suppose you can make a guess at to how much time?"

Time was of the essence, then. She made a mental note as she shook her head slowly. "I'd like to go into town, Bob. To the nearest store," she said, making up her plan as she went along, knowing full well Bob wasn't going to let her go anywhere. "I need to get some more supplies. Things that will help Jake to remember his past."

Bob shrugged. "You'd get lost for sure. There are a dozen turns between here and there, and not a road sign on any of them."

She'd counted on him saying something like that, but she sighed in disappointment all the same. "I suppose you're right."

"I know I'm right."

"Maybe I could just make you a list?" She smiled at him, holding his eyes, keeping hers trusting and hopeful.

He smiled back at her, looking smugly satisfied with himself for having fooled her yet again. "Sure. You just tell me what you need and I'll see to it."

She nodded. "Some clothes, for starters. I think he'll feel more like himself if we dress him in the things he used to wear. I don't suppose you kept any of his old stuff?"

"Uh, no. Eventually, we gave it away. That's why his room is so stark and empty."

"Do you remember the kinds of things that used to be in there? The kind of decorations he had on the walls? The kinds of books he liked to read, the sort of music he liked?"

He frowned, completely blank, but nodded anyway. "Sure I do. He was like a brother to me." He didn't list any of them, she noticed. Because he didn't have a clue, she thought. Still, she wanted him gone long enough for her to have time to do what she needed to do.

"That's going to be the key," she said. "We just feed him his old favorite foods, surround him with stuff from his past, so that he sees it, hears it, smells it, feels it all the time. This is going to help me get through to him faster than anything else will, Bob." She wasn't lying. Surrounding a patient in familiar things was part of her deprogramming treatment—

that, combined with long hours of therapy, mild hypnosis and tender care, were the thrust of what had become known as the Dalton approach. "We're getting closer," she said. "I just know we're getting closer."

He nodded, gnawing on his lower lip. "I don't know. Do you really think all this stuff will help?"

"I'm the world's leading expert on this sort of thing, Bob. Trust me, I know what I'm doing. After all, this is what your mother is paying me for." She got up, taking her cup with her, leaving Bob alone to mull it over.

As soon as the doc was out of earshot, Bob hurried out to the barn. Agnes had left strict orders that he was not to use the telephone in the house at all, because Dr. Dalton was smart enough to listen in and he wasn't smart enough to watch what he said.

He didn't like Agnes. He didn't particularly like Oliver, either, though his reasons were different. Oliver was a weak man. Without Agnes's constant prodding, bossing and griping, he would probably melt into a little puddle on the ground. He was weak and he was whipped. Agnes, on the other hand, was just evil.

But he was being paid good money to do what he was told and not ask questions. And so he would do what he was told. First and foremost, he was to keep the doctor and the patient here at the ranch by any means necessary up to and including murder, but only

as a last resort. They were not to get out of here alive.
The nightly injections should keep Jake immobile, in-
coherent, and the drug might help him to remember
whatever it was Agnes and Oliver were so eager for
him to remember. Second, Bob was to call Agnes the
second Jake got his memory back. He didn't know
what was to happen to the prisoners after that. He
could make an educated guess, though. He didn't really care, so long as he was paid on time.

But right now he needed instructions. So he went
out to the barn, opened the door of what looked like
a gray metal electrical box on the wall and used the
telephone there to call the emergency number Agnes
had left for him.

When they heard Bob's footsteps in the hall, Zach
lay back on his pillows and Maisy took away the
water she'd been making him drink almost nonstop
in an effort to flush the drugs from his system. She
yanked up the book of nursery rhymes, opened it at
random and began reading aloud.

"'Here I am, little jumping Joan. When nobody's
with me, I'm always alone.'"

She looked up in mock surprise when Bob poked
his head through the door, then smiled as genuinely
as she could manage. "He's listening, Bob. Your
mother was right about these nursery rhymes. I think
we're going to reach him soon."

Bob smiled back at her, and there was more than
friendliness in his smile. It made her cringe inwardly.

On a practical level, she supposed his interest was a good thing. It could be used to their advantage.

"That's great news. Listen, I'm going to go on into town to get those things you asked for." He glanced at Zach.

So did Maisy. He lay on the pillows, his head cocked to one side, eyes staring blankly at a spot on the wall, mouth slightly open.

"You gonna be okay alone with him?" Bob asked.

"I gave him a mild sedative a little while ago," she said. "He'll be out for hours. You couldn't have picked a better time to go."

"That's a relief." He smiled down at Zach. "Hey, pal, how are you feeling? Mom says you kids' bedrooms always smelled of violets. She says you had a purple teddy bear you used to sleep with. And you liked Mozart. Can you imagine that? A kid liking Mozart?" His eyes shifted quickly to Maisy's. "I mean, that was one thing I didn't remember at all. But I was pretty young, you know. Anyway, I figure I should be able to find at least some of those things to put around the room here."

Maisy nodded as if in approval. "Great. I think we'll see a breakthrough within another day or so. I really do."

"I shouldn't be more than an hour."

"I'll be fine until you get back."

He nodded and then left. Maisy waited, watching out the window as he got into the battered pickup truck, started it and drove away. Then she turned to

Zach. "Did you catch what he said? 'You kids' bed-rooms.' As if he were talking about Jake's siblings."

Zach frowned. "Makes...no sense."

"Why not? You're Jake's sibling, aren't you? Do you remember any of those things from when you and he were small children together?"

He shook his head slowly. "Jake...adopted at twelve."

She blinked. "Jake was adopted at the age of twelve?"

Zach nodded.

Well, that put a whole new spin on things. She glanced out the window again, just in case. "Okay, he's gone. Now I can get to the phone and get us some help. And then I'm going to search this place and find out where he's keeping the drugs he's been giving you and just what they are." She pushed the water pitcher closer to the edge of the stand. "How are you doing? Can you stay awake?"

He nodded.

"You watch for him. If he pulls in that driveway, you send that pitcher to the floor. I want to hear a loud crash, okay?"

Zach gave her a thumbs-up. His eyes met hers. "You're...something."

"So are you."

He held her gaze for a moment longer. She felt the pull of attraction, stronger than before, but forcibly ignored it. Finally, she turned and left the bedroom, leaving the door wide open.

The first place she went was to the wall phone in the kitchen. But when she picked it up there was no dial tone.

"I should have known," she muttered, replacing the phone, and closing her eyes. "God, Zach's right. We're being held prisoner here."

She shook herself and parted the curtains, looking toward her car. The dog lay sprawled between the porch and the driveway, and there was no chain holding him this morning. So much for Bob's promise to keep him away from her.

There seemed no escape from the farmhouse, but her search of it was a revelation. The living room and kitchen looked lived in, but many other rooms in the place were as dingy and dusty as if they hadn't seen life in twenty years. Peeling wallpaper, cracked plaster, cobwebs were everywhere. For the first time she noticed, really noticed, that all the rooms that *did* look lived in—or maybe all the rooms they expected her to see—had been recently fixed up. Aromas of fresh paint lingered in the air. The curtains were so crisp and spotless they had to be new. The sofa still smelled of stain-protectant.

The place was like a film set. No coffee rings on the furniture, no months-old magazines piling up in a corner. Nothing to say anyone actually lived here, or had for more than a few days.

She went through every cupboard, every drawer and every room of the house. The downstairs bathroom, which was off the dining room, had brand-new fixtures—a shower stall, toilet, a basin with shiny new faucets. It was the room Bob had gone into when he'd fetched the first-aid supplies for her dog bite. The walls were dingy and the floor creaked when she stepped on it, but the water ran hot and cold.

She searched the bathroom thoroughly, certain she would find whatever drugs they'd been injecting into Zach's poor body. But no. There was nothing to find.

After searching every last room of the place and finding nothing else, Maisy returned to the living room and sank onto the sofa, sighing in defeat. Where the hell did Bob sleep? And what about Agnes and Oliver when they were in residence? There wasn't another habitable bedroom in the place.

She sat there, frowning, mulling and shifting her bottom away from the lump that was poking her.

Then she paused. Everything here was new, including the sofa. Why would there be a lump?

Jumping to her feet, she yanked off the cushions. It was a sofa bed. She dragged the coffee table out of the way and quickly unfolded the convertible sofa. Its mattress was all made up, sheets, blankets and pillows in place. And there was a small plastic box there, folded up in the center. Maisy opened it, seeing just what she had expected to see: three tiny glass vials and a pile of plastic-wrapped, disposable hypodermics. She picked up a vial, reading the label.

Sodium Pentothal. Known in some circles as truth serum.

That was what they'd been doping Zach with? My

God, she could only hope they hadn't done any permanent damage to his brain.

She took one of the cellophane-wrapped hypodermics, hoping to God Bob hadn't counted them, and set to work.

It was going to take time. She could only hope Bob would stay away long enough.

Bob wasn't gone long, but Zach heard the woman's footsteps coming up the stairs just as he reached for the pitcher to sound the warning, so he waited. She came into the room.

God, she was pretty. Even now that his head was starting to clear a little more, thanks no doubt to the untainted food and water she'd been providing, she still looked to him like an angel. Oh, he didn't hear the wings fluttering anymore, but she still had that glow about her. He'd always had a weakness for brown-eyed girls, and her eyes were the biggest, prettiest, brownest pair he'd ever seen. She stepped into the room, closing the door behind her.

"He's back," Zach said.

She frowned, hurrying closer to the window and glancing out. "It's all right. The phone's out, but I found the drugs and—"

The front door banged. "Dr. Dalton?" Bob called.

She sighed and went to the door. "Up here, Bob," she called. Then she turned to Zach and whispered, "I'll fill you in later. For now just trust me and follow my lead."

The man's heavy feet were already banging up the stairs. He came into the bedroom, a couple of shopping bags in his arms. Maisy looked intently at Zach, then flicked a finger over her eyes in the split second before Bob looked at either of them.

Zach thought he got it. He closed his eyes promptly.

"Any trouble?" Bob asked.

"He's still sleeping. I just wish I knew why."

"Just as well, I guess. I got some of the things you asked for." There was the rustling of bags. "I got this little pot. You put a candle in the bottom and it heats up the water in the top."

A potpourri pot, you idiot, Zach thought in silence.

"The woman at the store said to put a little water in the top part, and drop some of this violet oil into it. She said petals would work, too, but they didn't have any of those." More rattling. "Here are the candles for it. I picked up a portable CD player and a couple of the CDs you asked for. Mozart. And, uh…" more rattling "…this."

"Ohhh," Maisy said in a long, drawn out, isn't-that-precious sort of way that convinced Zach he had to peek.

He opened one eye, just a little. She was taking a soft brown teddy bear with shiny brown eyes from Bob, and she was smiling. "This is so cute." She held the thing as if it were a child.

"They didn't have any purple ones."

"You did great, Bob. I know this stuff will help, if I can just get him to wake up."

He glanced in Zach's direction, and Zach closed his eyes again. "You must be hungry. You want some lunch?"

"Sure. You know, I'm surprised the hospital lab hasn't called by now. I'm dying to see what that blood work turns up."

"Yeah, me, too."

Zach felt the touch of something incredibly soft near his face and realized the doc was tucking that foolish little bear beside him. Then he listened, peeking now and then while she set the mini—boom box on the floor beside his bed and plugged it in, sticking in a CD and setting its volume low. She put water in the little potpourri burner and set it on the nightstand.

"Best not light the candle just yet," Bob said. "Not when he's alone in the room, anyway."

"Good idea. You're so smart, Bob." She poured a few drops of violet oil into the pot. Zach could smell it even without the candle burning. Sweet, but strong. Kind of like the woman he was becoming a little bit more than fond of. And he did not like the idea of her leaving the room in Bob's company. The big guy was looking at her way too closely, way too speculatively.

"Let's get that lunch," she said. She held the door, not leaving the room until Bob did. Not giving him a chance to be alone with Zach. My God, she was protecting him.

Zach was a liberal thinker, a modern educated man. But it still made him squirm a little to have a small, beautiful woman squaring off against a dangerous criminal in order to save him. It tormented him almost as much as seeing her face the killer dog outside had done. He had already harbored doubts about his own heroic qualities, an area in which he feared he was sadly lacking. Jake was the heroic one in the family. He was more athletic, more outgoing, more aggressive. Zach had always been the bookworm.

Now, as if to drive the point home, he was being rescued by a woman. He wasn't sure his ego would get through this unscathed. But he was sure he needed her. He didn't stand a snowball's chance in hell of getting out of here without her help. He would just have to worry about his male pride later. When he was free, and the drugs they'd been slipping into his food and injecting into his body had worn off more completely.

More than his own self-image, more than survival or escape, he kept thinking about how he must look to Maisy Dalton, and whether she saw him as some kind of helpless wimp. She didn't show any signs of seeing him that way.

He certainly didn't want her to see him that way.

The way he *did* want her to see him, when he gave it any thought, surprised him. He wanted to be the hero. He wanted to rescue her from this mess. And he wanted her to feel as attracted to him as he felt to her.

The very fact that he was even thinking about that sort of thing at a time like this was enough to tell him he had it bad. This woman hit him like no woman ever. It wasn't just the drugs. He knew it.

Seven

Jake Ingram sat back from his desk and rubbed his eyes. He had been staring at computer screens all day, working to trace the electronic trail of the billions stolen from the World Bank. It was elaborate work, the person behind it a computer mastermind the likes of which he'd never encountered. Never.

And that worried him. The same way it seemed to be worrying most of the world at this point. It was clear that a person capable of hacking into the World Bank's top-notch computer system, despite its state-of-the-art security features, could just as easily penetrate that of any company in the world.

People were scared, and this was only the beginning. The potential worldwide repercussions of this crime were staggering.

More staggering, though, was the knowledge that the genius behind this could just as easily hack into other systems: air-traffic control, the military, the government. He could potentially start World War III with the click of his damned mouse, and Jake was plodding along, trailing him byte by byte.

He got to his feet, paced the office. Little dots

danced in and out of his vision. Eyestrain. Not the first time.

Finally, he reached for the phone and dialed his brother's number. He'd called Zach a couple of times already, but never seemed to catch him in. Then he'd get so overwhelmed with the job he would forget to follow up.

He needed an objective eye, and while all of his work was strictly hush-hush, he trusted Zach like he trusted no one else. Even though Jake was adopted, Zach had never once made him feel like an outsider— he'd been Jake's brother from day one. Besides, there was no one else he could talk to about the odd dreams. He thought they must have something to do with the stress of this job and the pressure he was under. Or maybe with that cryptic note he'd received telling him that his life was a lie. He had no memory of his life before his adoption into the Ingram family. More than stress, more than the note, he felt in his gut that the dreams had something to do with his forgotten past. He just wished he could make sense of them.

He'd been an only child, his adoptive parents had told him. He'd suffered trauma-induced memory loss when his birth parents had died in a terrible automobile accident, and he'd been placed with the Ingrams shortly thereafter.

The dreams, though, didn't quite match up with that. He kept seeing himself in a room with other children—several other children, though he never could wake with an exact number in mind. He saw their faces in the dreams, heard their laughter. He would wake with names hovering just on the edge of his consciousness. There were toys in the dreams, toys he couldn't have had, because they didn't exist back then. Child-size computers, books that read aloud to you when you touched the words printed on the page, electronic games that made even today's models pale by comparison. There was a bear of a man who was always playing with them, and a beautiful, gentle woman who always smelled of flowers. He'd been so obsessed with the dream he'd actually stopped by a perfume counter one day, sniffing scents until he found the one that matched what he recalled in the dreams. Violets.

Just like that cryptic note.

He needed his brother. He needed Zach.

But Zach's phone rang and rang. The machine picked up, and Zach's voice told Jake to leave a message. Then there were a series of beeps, one for each message already on the machine. They went on longer than he expected, and by the time they stopped, Jake was really worried. For the first time, he wondered why Zach hadn't returned his last few phone calls. Then he sat there a moment, mentally backtracking, and going stiff when he realized he hadn't heard from his brother in at least four days.

Hell! He hung up the phone, grabbed his coat and his keys, shut down his computer and headed for his brother's place. It wasn't like Zach not to return phone calls for days on end. Something was going on, and Jake could have kicked himself for not realizing it sooner.

Zach napped fitfully, and when he woke, it was with a start that set his pulse to pounding. But no one was there, and the room was dark.

"Doc?" He sat up a little in the bed, feeling stronger than he had before. Not full power, not yet. But he was gaining. Maisy was doing a good job seeing to it he didn't get drugged again. Maybe by tomorrow he would be able to get up out of this bed and be some kind of help in his own rescue.

He heard water running. Why the sound took so long to register on his brain was just one more sign of the state he was in.

There was light spilling in from the open bathroom door, and the shower was running. He frowned, tugged back his covers. "Doc, you in there?"

He didn't shout. Didn't want to alert Bob to the fact that he was awake and lucid, when Bob seemed to want him drugged to capacity, twenty-four–seven. Zach was dreading the man's return tonight, and he would return—Zach knew he would. He came every night.

Zach slid his feet to the floor, put a little weight on them, and when his legs held, he tried a little more. When he got upright, he swayed as dizziness hit him like a tidal wave, but he held on to the bed and managed not to fall to the floor. Taking a deep breath, he closed his eyes, waited for the dizziness to pass. It did, slowly, gradually.

When he thought he could balance, he tried walking, one unsteady step, then another, taking him on a meandering and slow-motion journey across the bedroom. He was panting and breathless when he finally reached the bathroom, and clung to its door frame to keep himself upright. He let his head hang forward, breathing fast and waiting for his pulse to stop hammering in his ears. Damn, he was weak.

When he could breathe enough to speak, he lifted his head and looked toward the shower. The water was still running, the frosted glass door closed. Beyond it, he could see the hazy outline of a female form, a peach-toned silhouette against the glass.

He swallowed hard and felt a stirring of pure male appreciation before he forced himself to lower his gaze. She was moving around in there beneath the spray. She was all right, and that was all he needed to know. He got himself turned around, and started back across the room, toward the bed. And he damn near made it, too. He was halfway there when his knees buckled and he sank slowly, soundlessly to the floor, out of energy. Then he lay there, wondering why he didn't hear the water anymore. He managed to roll over onto his back in time to see Maisy hurrying toward him.

"Zach!"

She was there a second or two after he fell, leaning over him, her hair dripping water all over his face.

He looked at her in the light from the bathroom. She'd grabbed her robe and thrown it on, but the water on her skin made it damn near transparent, and it clung. The sleeve was still torn from the dog bite, but she'd found time at some point to rinse the bloodstains away.

"Zach?"

His eyes, he realized, were pretty much fixed on her breasts. That probably wasn't altogether polite. But at least he was now reassured that certain bodily functions were rapidly returning to normal. Thank God. He'd have hated to see her this way and been unable to appreciate it.

He forced his eyes to focus on her face. Beads of water clung to her cheeks and her eyelashes. Her hair wasn't pinned up, but hung over her shoulders, long and slightly curly and very wet.

"What are you doing out of bed?"

"Checking on you," he told her. "I got worried."

She smiled just a little. He thought he knew why. If she'd been in trouble, just what help did he really think he could be to her?

"You're speaking so much more clearly now."

"Am I?"

She nodded, kneeling on either side of Zach's legs, then sliding her arms under his. "Come on, I'll help you up."

She pulled, and he sat up, but then he stopped and couldn't seem to move. He was fixated on how close her mouth was to his, and suddenly overwhelmed by the urge to taste it.

She stopped pulling, met his eyes, at first with a question, and then with the slow understanding of what he was thinking. He lifted a hand to cup the back of her head.

She turned away, quickly releasing him and straightening. "Now that I think about it," she said, pretending that the almost-kiss had never happened, "you could probably manage to take a bath now, if you wanted to."

He frowned, his hand automatically going to his chin, where he felt more whiskers than he'd ever worn in his life. "I guess I need one. I must look like hell. Do I smell bad, too?"

She looked at him quickly. "No, why do you think— Oh." She licked her lips. "You're a patient, Zach. I'm your doctor. Granted, this situation is... unorthodox, but the same rules apply. Do you understand?"

"No. What rules are you talking about?"

"I'm not supposed to notice, or care too much, how you smell."

Reality dawned. "Oh. *That's* why you wouldn't let me kiss you just now? Not because I'm getting ripe, but because of some doctor-patient code of conduct or something like that?"

"Something like that."

"Then I *don't* smell?"

She looked down at him, seemed to take in his

teasing smile, and the tension eased from her brows instantly as she relaxed and returned it. "You're teasing me, aren't you? God, you really are feeling better."

"Yeah. I really am. Physically I'm amazed how weak I still am, but my head is finally clearing."

"That's wonderful, Zach. I'm so glad."

"Yeah." He let his smile die. "I'd better enjoy it while it lasts. Good old Bob will be back in here tonight, with another dose of whatever the hell it is he's been giving me."

He slid sideways, gripped the bed frame and pulled himself up to his knees. The doc reached for him, but he held up one hand, and she let him do it on his own. He managed to get to his feet, then sat on the edge of the bed, breathless.

Maisy hovered close by, ready to help. "Sodium Pentothal," she told him.

He frowned at her, still working on catching his breath. "Huh?"

"That's what Bob's been giving you. They used to call it truth serum. They obviously think you know something that you're either refusing to or are unable to tell them."

He nodded. "That makes sense. After he injects me, he questions me. So did Agnes before she took off."

"What kinds of questions do they ask you?"

He frowned, shaking his head slowly. "I can't remember, only that it was always the same questions.

Over and over. And Agnes would read stupid nursery rhymes to me, and my mind would start conjuring little cartoon characters in my head to go with the stories.'' He shrugged. ''I remember bits and pieces. There's something about Medusa, something about— the Extraordinary Five, and they always mention brothers and sisters.''

He lowered his head. ''That's about all I can remember.''

She stood there a moment, arms crossed over her chest in the damp robe. He wasn't able to keep his mind from guessing that she wasn't wearing anything underneath it, and from wondering what would have happened if she'd let him kiss her there on the floor a moment ago.

Hell, he probably wouldn't be physically capable of following through. But he could fantasize.

''Zach, they told me you'd lost your memory. That you had been involved in a cult, perhaps for years, and living on a compound, and that you've been brainwashed.''

''No. I've been teaching economics at Greenlaurel University. In fact, I'd just finished my last class for the week and was in my car in the university parking lot when these clowns pulled up behind me. It was Agnes, pulling a helpless old lady routine. She asked for my help, and when I got close enough to her car, good ol' Bob came up behind me, stuck me with a needle and shoved me into the back seat. The next thing I knew, I was here.''

Zach lowered his head to catch his breath, furious that even sitting up and talking could exhaust him.

"You want to lie down?" she asked, her hands going to his shoulders.

"I'm tired of lying down."

"All right. Okay."

He lifted his head again, met her eyes. "I'm sorry." His hand cupped her cheek. "You're my salvation, and I've got no reason to snap at you."

"You're frustrated."

"More than you know. But still, no more than you must be. How is your arm?"

She shrugged. "Zach, they keep calling you Jake. You say Jake is your brother...."

"Yes. Jake is my brother. We look so much alike that when people meet us for the first time, they are constantly confusing us."

Her brows rose. Pretty eyebrows, arched and silky. "That part, I don't understand. I thought you said that he was adopted."

"I did. It's just a fluke that we're so much alike, I guess. Or maybe that's why my parents chose him. I mean, they never said that was it, but Jake was twelve when we took him in. His parents had been killed in a car accident and the poor kid was so traumatized he couldn't even remember his life up to that point. It tormented him that he'd forgotten his own parents. I felt for him. Right from the start, we were close."

She blinked slowly. "Did you hear what you just said?"

He looked her in the eyes.

"They think you're Jake. And they're claiming you have memory loss. Zach, do you think there might be something in Jake's past, in his childhood, that's behind all of this?"

He thought on that for a long moment, then shook his head. "I don't think so. I mean, no one really knows about any of that, outside the family. I'm not even sure if he's told Tara."

Maisy lifted her eyebrows.

"His fiancée," Zach clarified. "Frankly, I'm convinced this has more likely got something to do with the World Bank heist. Jake's been brought in to help with the investigation."

"Yes, I remember now."

He looked at her questioningly.

"I'd just glimpsed the headline in the newspaper, where it said he was working on the case. I never got time to read the article—in fact, I brought it out here with me to read when I found some free time, but when I went to get it from my bag, it was gone."

Zach lifted his brows. "You think Bob rifled through your things and took it?"

"Either him or the tooth fairy."

Zach lowered his head, sighing, hating what he was about to say, because he liked being with this woman. And he would like to be the one to save her, but it was high time she saved herself. "Listen, Doc, there's no reason for you to hang around here any longer.

You have to get out. You can let someone know where I am and send them back for me.''

"As if they wouldn't move you the minute they realized I was gone.''

"At least you'd be safe.''

She shook her head firmly. "I wouldn't do that, Zach. I wouldn't leave you here. Not like this. No way. And besides, I couldn't even if I wanted to. Not with that Cujo wannabe outside the house, ready to rip me to pieces if I so much as stick my big toe out the door. And didn't you say you saw Bob tinkering with my car?''

He nodded. "Yeah. I did. He was underneath it, lying on his back, first in the rear and then in the front. I was pretty drugged out, but it looked like he was putting something on your car, near the gas tank.''

She shivered and rubbed her arms.

Zach glanced out the window. "There's the pickup, the one he drives. You could take that.''

"He keeps the keys with him.''

Zach sighed heavily. "I don't like this. I don't like you being in danger because of me. Especially when they keep me so doped up I couldn't help you if I tried. God, when I saw that dog lunging for you—''

"Don't.'' She put a hand on his shoulder. "None of this is your fault. And if it happens again, you'll be able to come to the rescue. The drugs aren't going to be a problem anymore.''

He frowned at her. "What do you mean?''

"I told you I found his stash. I used one of the hypodermics to empty every vial. Then I refilled them with saline solution. Sterilized water and a little salt. It's homemade, but it won't hurt you. I put everything away exactly as I found it. Bob will never know I made the switch."

"So when he comes in here to inject me to-night—"

"You need to pretend it's real. Play the role. And be convincing. As long as we can keep Bob believing that you're too drugged to be a threat, and that I'm still buying the story, we'll be safe. And in the mean-time, you'll be getting stronger."

"And when I am? What then?"

"I haven't thought that far ahead." She looked into his eyes, her gaze touching him like a caress. "I only know that when I leave here, I'm taking you with me. We go together or not at all."

He lifted a hand, smoothed it through her hair. "You're a hell of a woman, Doc. Anyone ever tell you that?"

She smiled at him, very softly. "My husband. All the time."

His hand stilled, and he slowly drew it away. "Then I'm out of line. Sorry, I didn't realize—"

"He died three years ago, Zach."

He felt her pain and wished it wasn't accompanied by a little rush of relief. But he couldn't deny being glad the doc wasn't married. "What kind of man was he, your husband?'' he asked. It was an impulsive question, but he found he really wanted to know.

"An intellectual. A psychiatrist, like me, though his practice was more orthodox than mine. He provided therapy to troubled patients.''

"And that's not what you do?''

"No. I specialize in hypnosis, memory loss and deprogramming.'' She turned away and began to fuss with the items on the bedside stand. It seemed to Zach that she was uncomfortable talking about herself this way. And she seemed to have forgotten that she was still wet and barely dressed. He hadn't. Not for a second.

"What happened to your husband, Doc?''

She lowered her eyes, and her hands went still. "I don't...talk about that.''

"No? Not even with me?''

She looked up slowly, searching his eyes. "He'd been having an affair with one of his patients and had tried to end it. I believe that she couldn't handle losing him, and when they were in her car together, she drove it off the road, over a seventy-foot drop and into the ravine below. They were both killed. It was ruled an accident, but I'm certain it was a murder-suicide.''

He was stunned. Both at the story, and at the tears running slowly down her cheeks as she told it. "My God," he whispered. "I'm sorry. I'm so sorry, Maisy.''

She shrugged, sniffed. "Doctors, especially psychiatrists, shouldn't get involved that way with their patients. It's unfair, so very unfair in so many ways. It's a breach of trust, an abuse of power. And it always leads to disaster. Usually just for the patient, but sometimes for the doctor as well.''

He got it. He got it now. She *was* uncomfortable talking about herself with him. And she was also attracted to him. He'd seen it in her eyes, felt it in her touch. So she was letting him know, in no uncertain terms, that nothing was going to happen between them. And she was giving him what she probably thought was the world's best reason.

''You should lie down,'' she said. ''Bob might be up anytime, and I—'' She glanced down at herself, remembering at last what she was wearing. ''I should go put on something dry and run a comb through my hair.''

She got up and started out of the room.

''Doc?''

''Yes?'' she asked without turning.

''You know that I'm not who they think I am. I haven't spent any time at any cult compound, and I haven't really lost my memory or been brainwashed or anything even remotely like that. You know those things, you believe me about those things, don't you?''

She turned slowly. ''Yes, Zach. God, have you been doubting that? I'm sorry I didn't make it clearer. I do—I believe you. What I can't believe is that they thought they could fool me.''

"Good." He nodded slowly. "I thought you did, but I wasn't sure."

"I do. I doubted myself at first, but how could I have any question after I found the drugs?" She shook her head. "You don't have to worry, Zach. I'm good at my job, and it's clear to me that you're the one telling the truth."

He sighed as if in relief. "I'm glad. So then we're clear on this. You are *not* my doctor. And I am *not* your patient."

Her eyes widened a little. Her lips parted, as if she was about to argue with him, but then she closed them, turned and hurried through the bathroom and into her own bedroom, out of sight.

Eight

Jake Ingram arrived at his brother's place, a brownstone duplex near the university, and went to the door. He rang the bell repeatedly and tried the knob when no one answered, but the place was locked. Four daily newspapers lay on the front steps. Four. And the mailbox mounted to the wall beside the door was stuffed to overflowing.

Jake swore and reached for the spare key his brother kept in a potted plant near the door, then used it to enter, and searched the house. Zach wasn't there, but Jake had guessed as much when he'd seen no sign of the car in the driveway. The next logical place to check was the university, so he relocked the house, pocketing the key, and headed back to his car to drive there.

It was fully dark, but the parking lot was well lit, and Zach almost always parked in the same spot. Sure enough, Jake found his brother's car right there where it should be. The engine was cold, and nothing he could see inside the locked car told him anything. But then his foot hit something that jangled and he glanced down to see what it was.

A set of keys just underneath the car, behind the front tire. He picked them up quickly and saw the gold key ring with Zach's initials engraved in its face—the key ring Jake had bought him the day Zach had passed his driver's test and earned his license almost twenty years ago. God, they'd been so young.

Jake pulled his cell phone out of his pocket and dialed the number of the federal agent with whom he was working on the World Bank heist investigation.

The man answered on the second ring. "Lennox here."

"Something's happened to my brother."

The man paused. "Ingram? Is that you? What are you talking about?"

"My brother hasn't answered his phone in days. I went by his house and there are newspapers and mail piled up and no sign of him. His car is in the lot at the university where he teaches, and his keys are on the ground beside it. Something's happened to him. I know it. And if you want me to help you find your damn money, you'd better be willing to help me find my brother."

"Is this the brother who looks so much like you? The one with you in that photo of the fishing trip on your desk?" Lennox asked.

"Yes. His name is Zach." He swallowed hard. Just saying his brother's name made his throat tighten with emotion. Zach was more than his brother. He was Jake's best friend.

"I'll meet you at your office in an hour."

Jake pressed the kill button and walked slowly back to his car.

Maisy was determined to remain awake, so she could observe everything that might go on in Zach's room tonight. She wasn't about to let anything happen to the man.

And that, she assured herself, had nothing to do with the fact that she was drawn to him. Powerfully drawn to him. So powerfully that it felt as if he exerted some invisible tug on her senses and her emotions whenever she came within his range. She wasn't supposed to feel that way, not about anyone—and especially not about a patient.

His argument that he wasn't her patient wasn't a valid one. Not really. He'd been dosed with mind-altering drugs for days on end. He couldn't possibly be thinking clearly. It was her job to help him get clear—not clutter up his mind or give him even more to deal with, or take advantage of his condition to satisfy her own needs.

Even if they were needs she'd convinced herself didn't exist in her. She wasn't like other women, she'd decided. She didn't need a man to find her attractive in order to feel pretty. She didn't need a man's touch, or crave a man's kiss, or hunger for a man's arms around her. She didn't need to be loved or desired. She didn't need any of that.

She wasn't a shrink for nothing. She knew where

this sudden flood of strange emotions was coming from. She was struggling to stay afloat among them. Her intense physical attraction to the man was at the top of the list, sitting right beside her almost fierce drive to protect him, and her ever-growing mountain of guilt. Guilt for warming at the touch and tingling at the soft voice of a patient. Guilt for feeling things toward him she had never felt toward Michael. They'd been intellectual equals, friends, lovers, but they had never sizzled. Never torn each other's clothes off in the heat of passion. Their desire had been a cool, but steady flame.

She wondered sometimes what Michael had found with that troubled young woman, Kelly Monroe, that had drawn him so powerfully as to make him break his marriage vows. Had it been something like this thing she was feeling now for Zach Ingram? A physical, chemical attraction almost too potent to resist?

She had never before understood Michael's cheating on her. It had broken her heart when he had come to her and confessed. Now, at least, she thought she had some idea what he'd felt for the other woman. Because she felt it for Zach. Though in her case, the outcome would be far different. She would never give in to it. That kind of attraction was dangerous.

She would never, never understand, though, what Kelly Monroe had felt for her Michael that had driven her to kill him and herself, rather than let him go.

Sighing, Maisy rolled over and punched her pillow into a more comfortable shape. She hadn't tortured herself with thoughts about Michael and Kelly and their fiery, dramatic deaths for more than a year. Why the hell was she doing it now?

Well, one thing was for sure. She'd have no trouble staying awake tonight.

She glanced at the clock's luminous green digits: 12:07. Then she heard a sound. Footsteps on the stairs, heavy ones trying hard to be light. "Showtime," she whispered.

A key scraped in the lock on her bedroom door before it opened a crack. She lay on her side, facing it, her eyes closed lightly, breathing deeply and evenly, and she hoped she made a convincing show of being sound asleep, even though her heart was using her rib cage as a punching bag.

She must have, because her door closed again and the footsteps moved along the hallway. A second later, she heard Zach's door open. Her stomach clenched as she thought how frightening it must be for him to lie there in that bed, pretending to be asleep, and just waiting for Bob to do his worst. She hoped she had been correct in her guesswork, and that Bob wouldn't simply decide to kill Zach tonight.

She slid out of her bed, wearing a nightshirt, and a pair of ankle socks she hoped would muffle her footsteps. Quickly, she shoved her pillows beneath her covers in a rough approximation of a human being and then she padded into the bathroom. She'd left Zach's door to the bathroom open just a crack and had closed her own, and she hoped Bob wouldn't make anything of it. He ought to think she believed his story about Zach standing over her bed with a knife in his hand, and assume that she was taking precautions.

She hurried into the bathroom, leaving the light off, closed and then locked the door to her bedroom. Quickly she crossed to Zach's door and peered into his room.

Bob was leaning over Zach in the darkness. His hulking silhouette over Zach's bed made her pulse pound, and for an instant she thought of walking up behind him and cracking his skull with some heavy object.

But that wasn't the plan.

Zach struggled a little when Bob's hands closed on him. Maisy tensed, hoping it was part of the act, as they'd discussed. He resisted every night, so he should do the same tonight. Bob's hand was clamped over Zach's mouth, while his other hand stabbed a hypodermic into Zach's upper arm with all the gentleness of a bulldozer. Zach tensed, then stopped fighting, relaxing back into the bed.

Bob straightened, dropped the needle into the small bag he'd brought into the room with him, and then turned toward the bathroom.

Maisy ducked back, stepped into the shower stall and closed the door. She'd swung the hinged door open and closed several times earlier tonight, just to be sure she could do so silently. She had wiped the tub dry in preparation and had piled some folded towels on the bottom. She sank onto them carefully, scrunching low so Bob wouldn't see so much as her shadow through the frosted glass, even if he turned on the bathroom light to check.

Of course, if he opened the glass door...

She waited as his booted feet crossed the bathroom to her bedroom door. He tried the knob; she heard it jiggle just a little. Then he unlocked it, opened the door and, she guessed, peeked into her bedroom.

She gathered that the mound of blanket-draped pillows convinced him she was still sound asleep when she heard him close and lock the door again. He turned to walk toward her, closer to the shower stall. And closer. He stopped near the stall, and she clenched her jaw, fisted her hands and waited for the door to swing open.

Then he kept walking, back through Zach's door, pulling it shut behind him.

Maisy sighed in a relief so intense it made her dizzy. Then she got to her feet with excruciating care, opened the glass door the same way and stepped out of the tub. She crept to Zach's door and pressed her ear to the wood.

"Jake," Bob was saying. "Can you hear me, Jake?"

"Mmm."

There was a light smacking sound. Maisy frowned, quickly turning the doorknob and opening the door just a crack so she could see what was going on.

Bob was smacking Zach's face lightly with his palm. "Jake. Wake up. Talk to me."

"I'm 'wake," Zach muttered.

"Good." Bob was bending over him again, and Maisy realized he was binding Zach's poor arms to the bed frame, just as he had before. Then he went to the foot of the bed and used the crank there to raise Zach's body into a sitting position. "I need to ask you some questions, Jake. Okay? Maybe you'll remember something this time."

"Mmm."

Bob pulled something out of his bag, fiddled around for a moment, and then a blindingly bright light flashed on, so suddenly it startled her. He aimed it right at Zach's face.

Zach closed his eyes.

"None of that now." Bob returned to Zach, and she could see what he was doing much more clearly now. He peeled strips of adhesive tape from a roll and taped Zach's eyes wide open so that blinding light shone right into them. He put a strip of duct tape around Zach's forehead and the headboard to keep him looking straight ahead.

Oh, God. This was torture.

Bob went to the mini–boom box that was set up on the floor, and turned it on, adjusting the volume until Mozart was playing. Then he stuck a wire into the box that made the music go silent. A second later, he was sticking the other end of that wire into Zach's left ear. A single earphone. He poked it tight and used more tape to keep it there. Then he lit the candle beneath the potpourri, adding more violet oil to the water. And finally he took a small tape recorder from the bag, depressed a button and spoke into it. "Jake Ingram interview, day five." He set the device on the nightstand on the righthand side of Zach's bed and sat down in the chair there.

"All right now, Jake, it's time to remember." He spoke into Zach's right ear, leaning close. "What's your name? Hmm? Come on. Tell me your name."

Zach said nothing.

"Where do you live, Jake?"

"I…Greenlaurel, Texas," he said, slurring his words.

"No, not now. Before. Long, long before. Where did you live then?"

No answer.

"Come on, Jake, don't make me pull out all the stops. Do you have brothers and sisters? What are their names?"

"I…don't know."

Bob sighed. He got up from his chair and touched a button on the lamp. It began flashing, different colors each time, and it seemed to get even brighter. It hurt Maisy's eyes to look at the light, and she knew it must be killing Zach. Then Bob bent to the boom box and turned the volume knob.

Zach's face contorted, his unnaturally wide eyes straining to close, and he moaned.

"Come on now, Jake," Bob said, returning to his spot on the right, speaking into his other ear. He would have to, Maisy thought. The tinny music was so loud she could hear it without an earphone. "Tell me about your family," Bob said. "Tell me about the Extraordinary Five."

Maisy backed away from the door and looked around the bathroom for a weapon. No way was she going to stand here and watch Zach be tortured like this. Her stomach was heaving and her eyes burning. She found nothing and decided she'd just make do with her hands. She opened the door.

Bob's back was toward her, but Zach saw, somehow, despite the blinding light in his eyes. He managed to shake his head, just barely, against the tape that held it.

"No," he muttered. "No, don't do it."

"Don't do what?" Bob asked.

"Don't...make me remember!" Zach replied, probably latching on to the first thing he could think of. Then he rolled his eyes back in his head and let his jaw go slack, even as Maisy forced herself to back away, into the bathroom. She pulled the door closed almost all the way, her hands shaking badly.

"Jake?" Bob leaned in closer. "Jake, come on." He smacked Zach's cheek a few times, swore under his breath and smacked him harder. Then he checked for a pulse.

It made her shudder to think that Bob knew his actions could result in the man's death, and yet he went ahead anyway.

Sighing, Bob picked up the tape recorder. "Patient has lost consciousness. Apparently the heavier dosage wasn't the best idea. We'll revert to the former dosage and try again tomorrow.''

Then he clicked off the recorder and tossed it into the bag. He went to the light, his movements across the floor jerky in the strobe effect, his color changing rapidly. God, it made her dizzy to watch. He hit the switch, and the light returned to a steady white glare.

He moved around the bed, to shut off the little boom box, then jerked the earphone out. Then he reached for the tape holding Zach's eyes open. He ripped it off in such fast, brutal motions that Maisy almost cried out. Zach didn't make a sound. Bob yanked the duct tape from Zach's head with just as little care.

Bob went to the small bag on the floor, dropping in the used tape and the tiny earphone. He blew out the candle in the potpourri pot, then flattened the pillows behind Zach's head and untied his arms, tossing the ropes into the bag as well. He finally turned off the lamp and carried it in one hand, and the bag in the other, out of the room.

Maisy waited, forced herself to wait—even though it nearly killed her, until she heard the thug's heavy steps on every last one of the stairs, and crossing the floor below them. Then she tiptoed through the darkness, nearly blind from the formerly bright light. She had to move slowly, and it seemed to take her forever to reach Zach's bed.

He was sitting up, his legs over the side, his hands pressed to his forehead. She slid her arms around his shoulders, cradling his head to her chest. "Oh, God, are you all right?" He was shaking all over. Her fingers stroked his hair, one hand smoothing over his back repeatedly. "Are you okay, Zach?"

"I can't see." He sounded panicky. "God, I can't see."

"That's normal, Zach. It'll come back. You're not blind, I promise."

"Are you sure?"

She nodded, her head so close to his he could feel the movement.

"God, I think I was better off going through all that drugged," he whispered. He twisted his arms around her waist, holding her tightly. "I'm okay, I think. My head is pounding, I can't see a thing, my ears are ringing and I think I've lost most of my eyelashes, but I'm okay."

She rubbed his back, holding him, soothing him. "Lie back on the bed and close your eyes."

He did so obediently, and she pulled the covers over him, even though she knew his shaking wasn't caused by cold or by fear, but by sensory overload. "I have some pain reliever in my room. It'll help the headache. I'll be right back."

She leaned down, kissed his forehead.

He cupped a hand around the nape of her neck before she could rise again, and lifted his mouth to hers. He kissed her lightly on the mouth. "Thank you," he whispered. Then added, "You taste salty. Are you crying, Doc?"

She ran a hand over her cheeks to wipe away her tears. ''That's not going to happen to you again, Zach. We're not going to stick around here and *let* it happen again.''

''You *are* crying.''

''I'll get the pain reliever,'' she said, and tiptoed back into her bedroom to do just that. While she was there, she righted her bed pillows, just in case. If she were to be caught in Zach's room, she could simply say she got up to check on him. Perfectly harmless.

Only she wasn't harmless. Tonight, while she'd watched helplessly as Bob tortured Zach Ingram, she had felt, for the first time in her entire life, capable of harming—perhaps even killing—another human being. It frightened her.

She was barely gone a minute, and when she returned, she tucked two tablets between his lips, cradled his head in her palm and lifted it while she held the water glass. As if he were helpless.

Hell, he wasn't feeling his best, but he was far from helpless. He started to sit up to prove it, but she took the glass away and pressed a hot, wet cloth to his aching eyes.

''Just relax,'' she whispered. When she used that soft, soothing, half whisper, he couldn't do anything but obey. ''He won't be back again tonight. If he had given you enough of that garbage that he felt the need to check your pulse, he must think he gave you enough to keep you out for a long time. God, the idiot could have killed you.''

"But he didn't." Zach sighed, letting the heat from the cloth soothe his eyes. "You know, Doc, you might have saved my life tonight."

He couldn't see her smile, but he thought he *felt* her smile. Maybe there was a bit of dope residue in those little bottles, affecting his brain. Her soft, firm hands were on his forearms now, rubbing away the soreness left by the ropes.

"Look at this. He didn't need to tie you that tightly. God, even if you were at full strength, he wouldn't have needed to tie you that tightly."

"Hey, now. I'm stronger than I look, you know."

A little breath escaped her, maybe almost a laugh. "How can you joke at a time like this?"

"I'm not joking. I really am stronger than I look."

She moved away, but was at the other side of the bed a moment later, rubbing the other arm. "You look plenty strong, Zach, and I think you know it."

"Just as long as you do."

Her hands left his arm and came to his head, fingertips gently massaging his temples. God, that felt good. "We have to get out of here, Zach."

"I know." He licked his lips and let himself relax under her ministrations. She had a touch that was magic. Soothing, healing, warm. "The problem is, I don't know where 'here' is."

"The middle of freaking nowhere. But I have directions from my place, and I hid them in my room in case Bob comes snooping again. We can follow them in reverse to get out.''

''How far?''

He heard her sigh. ''Two and a half hours, by car.''

''Let's see, that translates to, what, twenty-five years on foot?''

''We'd never make it on foot. Bob would catch us. He has a truck, don't forget.''

''If we leave now, we'll have a six-hour head start. He never comes in here more than once a night.''

''That you know of,'' she corrected. ''Every other time he's probably left you too drugged to notice whether he came back or not. Besides, you're not ready. You need more time without drugs. At least one more day. A few solid meals.''

''I'm not sure if I can take another round of twenty questions with that guy and his laser light show.''

She drew a breath, as if about to say something, then slowly let it out again.

''What?'' he said. ''You just thought of something. What was it, Doc?''

''It doesn't matter. I couldn't do it.''

''Leave me?''

''No. That hasn't crossed my mind, and it won't, so you can quit bringing it up.'' She sighed heavily. ''I just— I think our lives might be on the line here, Zach. Once Bob figures out that he has the wrong brother, I don't think he or Agnes or whoever is in charge of this mess will have any further reason to keep either of us around. And it's not like they can just let us go at that point. We'd be too dangerous to them. We can identify them, and this place."

He knew she was right. "I'd thought of the same thing myself," he said. "I was just hoping you hadn't."

"Didn't want to worry my little head about it?"

"*Pretty* little head," he corrected, trying for a teasing tone. He didn't feel her respond this time. He didn't sense a smile.

"We're fighting for our lives, then, not just our freedom." She said it slowly, thoughtfully. "There are two of us, and only one of him. At least until the other two get back."

Zach sat up slowly, peeling the rapidly cooling cloth from his eyes, and blinking at her hazy outline in the darkness. "Are you saying we should consider doing something to him?"

She sighed, lowering her head. "I can't believe the thought of violence against another human being is something I'm even capable of considering as an option. But I am. I'm ashamed of myself, Zach, but I am. When I was down there in the kitchen yesterday, I was noticing the big knives in the drawer, and...."

He thought she shivered. "If it needs doing, Doc, don't think for one minute I'm gonna leave it up to you."

She met his eyes. "Could you, though? Could you actually kill a man?"

He tried to hold her gaze, despite his blurred vision and the darkness. And as he did, he thought it wouldn't be tough at all to kill a man if he were doing it to save this woman's life. Maybe not his own, but for her—yeah, he could do it in a heartbeat. The realization surprised him. "Only as a last resort, Doc. Only as a last resort."

"I saved a vial of the Sodium Pentothal. We might be able to drug him instead."

"We'd need three guys to hold him down while we injected him. Unless we could convince a horse to sit on his oversize ass for us."

She gripped Zach's shoulder so suddenly it startled him. "That's it."

"What? You know where we can find a horse trained to do something like that?" He was kidding again, trying to keep the mood light.

He could tell by the urgency in her grip that she was dead serious.

"I know where we can find a horse. More than one of them, in fact. Right on this very ranch. Out in the barn, unless Bob was making that up, but I don't think he was. I smelled horse on him when he came back from doing his chores yesterday. Nothing smells quite like a horse, does it?"

"I don't know, does it?"

"That's how we're going to get out of here, Zach."

"On horseback?" he asked.

She nodded. "Do you ride?"

"Not since I was a kid. But it's not something you forget. You?"

"Not as often as I'd like, but to get out of here, I'll bet I can manage."

"Me, too."

She sighed softly. "That's it, then. We'll get through one more day in this hellhole. I'll try to scope out the horses. We'll squirrel away some supplies when he's not looking. Some food, water, matches, blankets. Then tomorrow night—"

"Tomorrow night, we ride," he said, thinking it sounded like something out of a Western movie. Maybe he was going to have his chance to test his heroic side, after all.

Nine

"How are you feeling this morning?"

Zach stirred awake at the touch of her soft hand on his face, the sound of her soft voice close to his ear. He opened his eyes and blinked her into focus. It was a relief that he could see her clearly. After last night he'd wondered if his vision would ever return to normal. She smelled good, he noticed. Freshly showered, her still-damp hair pulled into a ponytail.

"I didn't even hear you come in," he replied.

"I know. I hated to wake you when you were sleeping so soundly."

"I'm usually a light sleeper." It was almost an apology. "God, what time is it?"

"Come on, Zach. Your body has a lot of recovering to do. It's only 9:00 a.m. After last night, you should have slept until noon. I would have let you sleep longer, but I thought you might want to know that Bob and I are going to be out of the house for a little while. I convinced him to— Shh. Here he comes."

Bob's now familiar footsteps clomped up the stairs and along the hallway. Maisy leaned close. "I smuggled you up some breakfast. He thinks you're still only able to take protein shakes, and I thought it best to let him keep believing it. But there's a plate in my room. Top drawer.''

He nodded slightly, closing his eyes as the heavy steps paused outside his door. The door opened and he heard Bob come into the room. The man's presence pervaded the place. Zach knew when he came to the bedside, leaned over to check him out.

"It's as if he's still being drugged," Maisy said. "Whatever they gave him at that compound is taking a long time to work itself out of his system. I've tried and tried to rouse him, but he's out cold."

"And you think he'll be all right alone for a while?" Bob asked.

"If he holds true to form, he won't stir for a couple of hours yet. Certainly time enough for me to stretch my legs, get a little fresh air and spend a few minutes with you."

Her voice changed a little with that last phrase. It became softer, a little more friendly. God, was she flirting with Bob? Was *that* what she was doing?

She tucked the covers around Zach. "Besides, we can lock the doors. He's not going to be any trouble."

"I gotta admit, I'd enjoy the company."

"I'll enjoy it, too, Bob."

Again her tone was softer, sexier. Zach was dying to open his eyes to see if there was an accompanying look that went along with it, but he couldn't blow this. Still, he didn't think the doc knew just what she was playing with here.

"I didn't hear the phone ring last night," she said to the big lug. "Did the lab ever call?"

"No, not yet."

"Odd. I thought for sure they would have some results by now."

"We can call them, if you want," he offered. "Right after chores. But, uh, we'd better get to the barn first. It's already late."

"Okay."

The two of them left the room together. Zach heard the lock on the outside of his door slamming home. Then he listened for their steps on the stairs, her soft ones drowned out by the heavier thud of Bob's boots. They crossed the ground floor, and the screen door creaked and banged. Zach rolled to one side, so he could see them out the window once they cleared the porch. There they were. The doc was walking very close to Bob. Way too close, in Zach's opinion. And then Bob put a hand on her shoulder, as if to guide her around a hazard on the ground.

Bastard.

The dog came trotting across the lawn behind them. Maisy couldn't possibly see it, and it wasn't barking. Hell.

Zach threw off the covers and got up, flipped the latch on the window and opened it just enough so he could shout a warning.

But then the two turned, and Bob spoke a word to the dog even as Zach ducked to one side, out of their sight.

"My goodness, he seems so harmless now," the doc said.

Zach peered again, careful to keep himself hidden from view. The dog was sitting, its tail thumping the ground.

"You're safe so long as you're with me," Bob assured her. "I know how to manage him."

Figured, Zach thought. One cur to another.

"It takes a special man to manage a dog like this one," Doc said. "Not many men could command respect the way you obviously do."

Oh, hell, she was flattering the guy. Zach's first assumption was right. She was flirting, on purpose. The woman was crazy.

"Do you think you could convince him to let me pet him?" she added.

An image of the doc's pretty hand being ripped from her forearm flashed into Zach's mind. But as he watched, Bob crouched down, held the dog's collar, patted his head and spoke to him, and the doc edged closer.

Zach could see the determination in her eyes, and he knew she had to be scared half to death. But she was completely in control—of both animals. She was crazy, all right. Like a fox. She moved closer to the dog, speaking softly, holding out her hand.

Zach wanted to do something, to stop her from taking such a risk, but he couldn't. He could only stand there and watch as she let her hand hover near the dog's deadly teeth. It sniffed her slowly.

"I was hoping you and I might be friends," she said softly. She drew her hand away, dipping into her jeans' pocket, and pulled out something wrapped in a tissue. "Here you go, boy. I saved this for you from breakfast."

Zach wasn't sure what she unwrapped or held in her open palm, but the dog ate from her hand, and its tail began thumping the ground even harder than before. Maisy patted the animal's oversize head and let it lick her hand clean.

"He's a good dog," she said. "Yes, he is. Rufus is a good dog. Yeah."

Bob was looking at her as if starting to realize that he'd made a serious mistake. He took her arm. "We need to get going. Rufus, go lay down. Go!" he said, pointing at the house.

The dog trotted off toward the house, its head hanging. Twice it paused to look back at the doc, wagging its tail both times. Zach sighed in relief and watched the two humans move out of sight, toward a barn in the distance, with Doc clutching Bob's arm and laughing over her success with the dog. Zach realized that she was executing a plan, and her plan was actually working. She was charming the hell out of both of them—the man and the canine.

He shouldn't be surprised, Zach supposed. He'd been charmed by her from the very first. *Charmed* wasn't exactly the right word, though. It was considerably more than that, and it grew with every minute he spent within range of her smile. She was smart. Braver than most men he knew. Beautiful. Kind.

She was also wounded and extremely fragile, much as she would prefer to keep that side of her hidden. And Zach found himself wanting to nurture and heal her, the way she'd been doing for him.

Now that she was no longer in his range of sight, he forced himself to stop thinking about his growing feelings for her and to take stock of his current situation. He'd jumped out of bed fast when he'd seen the dog rushing toward Maisy, but no rush of dizziness had swamped his head as a result. He moved his arms, his legs. They felt much closer to their normal state than they had in days.

Great. He only had a little time, and he was probably taking a huge risk, but he had to. He went directly to the bathroom and stripped off the pajamas he'd been wearing for the past several days. When he cranked on the taps and stepped into the shower's warm, welcome spray, he felt better than he had since the bastards had taken him.

He scrubbed himself from head to toe and washed his hair twice. Then he dried off and wrapped the towel around his hips. He ran some fresh water into the tub and dropped the pajamas in to soak. Bob hadn't looked into the bathroom before he'd left, and he hadn't checked under the covers to see what Zach was wearing. For all he would know, the doc could have given him a sponge bath and rinsed the pajamas out earlier in the day.

Zach was *dying* to shave, but that would be too obvious. In the medicine cabinet he found a new toothbrush, still in its wrappings, no doubt meant for him, and he made good use of it.

When he finished, he hung the now clean pajamas over the shower rack to drip dry. Then he used Maisy's hair dryer, which she'd left lying beside the sink. It wouldn't do for Bob to notice that his hair was wet when it had been dry before.

Then he tried the doc's bedroom door. Unlocked, as he had known it would be. Lured by the smell of the food she'd left for him, he went inside and found the wrapped plate tucked in an empty dresser drawer. The scrambled eggs, sausage and toast were still warm. She'd left a glass of juice out as well, by her bedside stand so it looked as if she'd been drinking it and had just left it unfinished. God, he was hungry. He downed every crumb of food.

Then he eyed the doorway to the hall.

Too tempting to resist. He had to get a look around this place. He was tired to death of being the helpless one, the invalid, while the doc did all the rescuing. She was damned good at it, clever and cunning, but he'd be damned if he would let her do all the work.

He stepped into the hallway, then stopped, listened, looked around. Only when he was convinced that the house was still empty did he move on, tiptoeing along the hallway and then, slowly, down the stairs.

"This is really a beautiful place," Maisy said, walking what turned out to be a well-worn path through a scraggly meadow to a sagging barn that was in need of a fresh coat of red paint. She walked closer to Bob than she needed to, brushed her shoulder or hip against his every now and then. It kept him off balance, and kept him from paying too much attention to whatever else she might be up to. She'd never had much confidence in her powers of attraction before, never even would have thought to use them as a weapon. Bob had given her the idea, just by looking at her too long or letting his eyes linger on parts other than her face.

Maybe the realization that Zach was attracted to her was lending her confidence in that area, too. His eyes, when he looked at her, held something above and beyond anything she might see in Bob's eyes. Bob was attracted, yes, in a predatory, "I've-been-too-long-without-a-woman" sort of way. But Zach— Zach looked at her the way some people looked at fine art and others looked at rainbows. He looked at her with wonder in his eyes, and caring, and desire, all mixed together to create a glow and an intensity that sent chills down her spine.

She shivered now, just at the memory of that look.

Having a man like Zach look at her that way made her feel more attractive than she had ever felt in her life. More capable, and more powerful, too. A man like Zach, she thought. A man so attractive and accomplished he could probably have any woman he wanted.

"The ranch isn't nearly what it ought to be," Bob was saying. She tried to force herself to at least pretend to be paying attention. "The pastures ought to be reseeded. They're mostly weeds. And the barn needs work."

"It's been hard without your cousin to help out, I'll bet." Maisy hoped she sounded sympathetic.

He glanced at her. "I do what I can. But it's more than one man alone can keep up." He shrugged. "Mostly, the ranching is just a front."

Her head came up quickly. Was he about to confess something? "A front?"

He nodded. "The few head we keep are only here to maintain the image. Dad doesn't want to let his old dreams go, and we don't have the heart to take them from him. But the truth is, this place costs more to run than it brings in."

"Oh. That's so sad. What do you live on?" She bit her lip as soon as she said it. "I'm sorry, that was a rude question."

"It's okay. I'm kind of flattered that you're interested. I actually made some savvy investments back when things were good. I've been siphoning my own funds into this place for years. And I do side jobs for other ranchers when things get particularly tight."

"You're a saint, to give so much to your family," she said, because it was perfectly clear that was the image he was trying to project. The self-sacrificing son, who was single-handedly saving the day for his parents.

"Nah, I'm just doing what any decent man would do." He nodded toward the tipsy-looking red barn just ahead of them. "Here we are." Then he gripped the handle of the sliding door and pushed it sideways. Its wheels ran on a rusty track, squealing in protest.

Reaching inside, he flipped a switch, and lights flashed on in the dim interior. She was surprised there was electricity in such a ramshackle building. But it was clean. The barn smelled of horses and hay. It was a good smell.

To the left were four stalls, each with a horse peering over the top of its door at her—a dirty white one with its mane hanging in its eyes, a dapple-gray that looked even older, a red-brown one with a spiky, short mane sticking up between its ears, and a darker brown one with a white diamond on its forehead.

Bob closed the barn door, then walked to the far end and opened a rear one just like it. Sunlight spilled in from outside. The dirty white horse nickered as he came back.

"What are their names?" she asked.

"Huh?" He glanced at her, then at the horses again. She realized they didn't have names; of course they didn't. They were props. They had probably been purchased recently and would likely be sold again the instant this little scam was over.

For the moment, though, he was struggling, and she needed to give him an easy out. Keep him placated. "Are you one of those ranchers who doesn't believe in naming his livestock?'' she asked in a teasing, friendly tone.

Relief washed over his face. ''Yeah. It's not like they're pets or anything.''

She nodded in agreement. ''Do you ride them?''

''Sometimes,'' he said.

She looked around the barn. ''I don't see any saddles or tack or— Don't tell me you ride bareback?''

''Sure. Why not?''

She smiled. ''My goodness, you are a man of many talents.''

He was opening the stall door at the far end. The dark brown mare came when he tugged on her halter, her swollen belly swaying with every step. Maisy would have commented on it, but she wasn't sure Rancher Bob was even aware the horse was carrying a foal.

As the mare walked toward the exit, Bob was opening the other stalls, one by one. The other horses exited the stalls and plodded toward the rear. The red-brown one, whom she was already thinking of as Spike, was a young stallion, full of fire. The dapple-gray appeared to be a gelding, and he had more spring in his step than the dirty white mare, which, Maisy guessed was beyond her breeding years.

In a line, the horses exited the barn, moving out the back and off to the left. Maisy hurried to the open door to see where they went. The pasture was fenced with new posts and new wire. It was large enough that she couldn't see its entire boundary.

Bob joined her in the doorway. "The cattle are over that way," he said, pointing to the right of the barn. That pasture was huge as well, also newly fenced and dotted with a half-dozen cows grazing eagerly on the stubbly, thin grass.

"The grass isn't very high just yet," she observed.

"No."

"You, um, feeding them anything extra?" She shouldn't have asked. It would not do to let on that she knew more about ranching than he did, much less that she suspected as much. But she'd been raised in ranch country. You didn't grow up surrounded by ranchers and not pick up a few things. She didn't want the poor animals to go hungry, either.

He glanced at her. "The horses get grain at night when they come inside. The cows stay out, but they have a feeder out there. I fill it every morning." He walked slowly back through the barn. "That's about it."

She looked around the place, nodding. "It's a nice enough setup."

"It works for us." He took a large square shovel from a hook on the wall.

"So what do you do now?"

"I clean the stalls, put fresh bedding in them. There's a pile of sawdust outside. They like that well enough. Then I'll take some feed out to the cattle, count 'em, check the fence, and unless there's a problem, that's it for the morning."

They were exiting through the front of the barn now. "You have a tractor around here somewhere?"

"No. Why?" He was frowning at her.

"You said you had to take feed out to the cattle."

He smiled a little, nodded toward one side of the barn. She saw a large wheelbarrow sitting there, and nodded in turn. "It's not exactly light work, is it, Bob?"

"It's nothing." He cleared his throat. "But it won't take me long."

His eyes were hinting at something, pinning hers and holding them. She was suddenly uncomfortable, and wondered if she'd played on his attraction a little bit more than was wise. "I, um, I should probably get back to our patient. You know, just in case."

He nodded. "I agree."

She waited, but he didn't say anything else, and didn't release her gaze until she lowered her eyes and started to turn away.

His hand snapped out to catch her upper arm. "Maisy?"

Sensing what was coming, she swallowed hard. But she turned slowly to face him again and kept her revulsion in check, never letting it show on her face. "Yes, Bob?"

"I, uh, I'll walk you back."

She smiled. "You're so sweet. But don't let me keep you from your work, Bob. I can find my own way."

"I'd hate to have anything happen to you." He slid

an arm around her shoulders, as if she'd given him permission to do that. Maybe he took her flirting as just that. He walked with her, very close to her, holding her against his side.

She tried to relax and smile, not to tense or pull away, as every instinct in her body was telling her to do. She tried to tell herself she was the one in control. He was reacting just the way she had wanted him to, albeit a little bit more quickly than she had anticipated.

"It gets lonely out here, Maisy," he said. "You must be getting lonely, too."

"Who wouldn't be?" she asked.

"Jake, he's no company at all, lying around in a stupor all the time."

"He'll get better, though. I just need time."

He nodded slowly. "To be honest, I don't know how much time they're going to give you. But when this is over…"

"When this is over?" she asked, turning to face him. They'd stopped walking, just a few feet from the porch, and she looked up at him now, certain he was about to reveal something, even if he didn't mean to. "What will happen then, Bob? When this is over?"

He stared at her for a moment, then sighed and pulled her closer, mashing his mouth to hers, kissing her hard and passionately, then letting her go while she was still reeling with shock. He stood there, searching her face as if waiting for some reaction.

"I…Bob, this is so sudden."

His eyes blazed and he reached for her again. But then a sound from inside the house, a banging sound, made him snap his head around, just as the dog came running out from underneath the porch to greet them, without a single growl or snarl.

Bob moved, but Maisy wrapped her arms around his neck and held herself against him, pressing her lips to his, hoping like hell to distract him.

He gripped her arms and removed them firmly, then stomped up the porch steps and flung open the door. "Jake?" he called.

She rushed in behind him. "Don't be silly, Bob. Jake couldn't get himself out of bed, much less down the stairs."

He ignored her, surging through the house and pounding up the stairs, with Maisy racing to keep up. "Honestly, Bob, I don't know what you're thinking."

He wrenched open the lock, flung the bedroom door wide, and rushed inside.

Zach lay in the bed, in exactly the same position he'd been in before—eyes closed, mouth slightly open, covers tucked around him.

"I know I heard something," Bob said.

"I heard it, too," Maisy replied. "But as I was trying to tell you before, it was Rufus. He knocked over his dish when he came running toward us."

Bob studied her face, his eyes narrow. "You saw it?"

"Of course I saw it. If I hadn't, I'd have been as worried about Jake as you were."

He studied her for a long moment, then finally sighed and relaxed. Stepping closer, he ran a hand through her hair. "I guess I was just a little tense."

Then he smiled as if to suggest she was to blame for that. "I'm gonna go finish those chores, and when I come back, I'll wash up, and you and I can pick up where we left off." His eyes, trailing down over her body, left no doubt as to what he had in mind.

"I can hardly wait," she whispered, but beyond Bob she could see Zach in the bed. His eyes were open, and they were furious.

"What the hell do you think you're doing?" he asked, barely managing to keep quiet until the door closed behind Bob.

"Shh!" The doc rushed to him, clapping a hand to his mouth and sending a petrified look back toward the door.

Zach could clearly hear the lug's thumping footsteps going down the stairs, and at this point he didn't really care. He shook off her hand and sat up in the bed. "Does the term 'playing with fire' mean anything to you, Doc? You are alone in the middle of nowhere with a criminal who's twice your size! Now he thinks you want to jump his bones."

"I'm not *alone* with him. You're here."

He blinked in shock, but it was lost on her. She was busy noticing his unclothed chest, now that the blankets had fallen to his hips. And he really liked the way she was noticing it.

"You're undressed," she said, her voice a little hoarse.

"I showered."

"My God, Zach, you took a terrible risk. What if he'd come back and caught you?"

"He didn't," Zach said. "I also brushed my teeth, washed the pajamas and took a tour of the house. Brought back a souvenir." He pulled the butcher knife from underneath his pillow as he said it. The doc went a shade paler and looked ill.

"I hope to God we won't need that."

"It's a better weapon than the one you're planning to use, Maisy."

She blinked at him, maybe a little bit confused by his anger. Hell, she should be. God knew he was. "What are you talking about?"

"Sex. If you think I'm going to let you bed that lug just to get us out of here, you'd better think again. I'd sooner stay where I am."

She lifted her brows. "I am *not* planning to 'bed' him, as you so colorfully put it."

"No? Then why is he looking at you as if he wants to eat you alive?"

She lowered her eyes from Zach's, and her cheeks turned red. "Because I flirted with him to get him to lower his guard."

"I think you did a little more than flirt." Zach was behaving like a pouting child and he knew it, but he couldn't seem to stop himself. "I saw you kissing him outside."

"If you hadn't made so much racket in here, I wouldn't have had to!"

He pursed his lips.

She pursed hers.

"You shouldn't have done it," he muttered.

Sighing, she sat on the edge of his bed. "Are you jealous, Zach?"

He glanced at her, raised his brows, because he was surprised at the directness of the question—and more so by the directness of his answer. "Yeah. I guess I am. I don't like him calling you 'Maisy' and thinking he has the right to put his hands on you."

Her lips pulled into a slight smile. "You can call me Maisy if you want to, Zach. But frankly, I kind of like when you call me Doc. I think it's sweet. And I never was overly fond of my first name, anyway."

"No?"

She shook her head. "No. I publish under my initials, M.J."

"For Maisy Jo?" he asked, his tone slightly teasing.

"Worse than that. Maisy Jane," she confessed.

He made a face, but then his expression grew more serious. "You let him kiss you," he said softly. "But you wouldn't let me. I guess my ego took a blow."

Her hand caressed his face, just lightly on one side. "I didn't want his kiss. I had to grate my teeth and force myself not to gag. I wasn't worried about his kiss making me lose my focus or my objectivity."

Zach locked his gaze on her, searching her eyes

and hoping she would keep being direct and honest. He loved that about her. "And mine would have?"

"Yours...I wanted. I had to fight as hard to resist kissing you as I had to fight to force myself to kiss him."

He held her eyes, grateful for her forthright explanation. She was blushing a little, but her gaze never wavered. "I appreciate you telling me that...."

"But...?" she asked, clearly picking up on the fact that he'd stopped before he'd said all that he was thinking.

He smiled. "But I'd have preferred the kiss."

She shook her head slowly. "Not gonna happen."

"Yeah, I think it is. I know this isn't the time, and it sure as hell isn't the place, but—"

She lowered her head. "I can't, Zach."

"Because of your husband?" She just shook her head. "Come on, Doc, you've been straight with me so far. Don't stop now. Tell me why."

There was a long exhalation, a slow lowering of her lashes to sweep across her cheeks. "I just...I can't go through it all again, Zach. The trust, the betrayal, the loss. The heartbreak. It almost killed me. I can't go through it again." She lifted her eyes to his, and they were wet, and her tears were like blades driven straight through his heart. "Can't we just be friends?" she asked, her voice choked.

He lifted his hand to brush a tear from her cheek with his thumb. He didn't really think they could be friends, because he'd made up his mind that they were going to be more than that, much more. He'd been waiting all his life for a woman who made him feel the way Maisy did. He knew there was more to come than the cool, comfortably friendly relationships he'd had with other women. He'd seen it—but never felt it. At least, not until now. But maybe now wasn't the time to tell her these things. God forbid he do or say anything to cause one more tear to fall from those brown eyes. "I'll take what I can get, Doc."

"Thank you for that."

He swallowed hard and forced himself to let it go for now. "Now, just what do you think Bob meant when he said you could pick up where you left off when he comes back from the barn—and how are we going to avoid it?"

Ten

Jake fought his way through the throng of reporters outside his office, most of whom shouted questions that he had no idea how best to answer.

"Mr. Ingram, is it true that your brother is missing?"

He held up a hand and kept walking. Cameras flashed, blinding him.

"When's the last time you saw your brother, Mr. Ingram?"

"Is this the same Zachary Ingram who teaches economics at Greenlaurel University?"

He shouldered his way up the steps, biting his lip.

"Do the police suspect foul play?"

"Could this have anything to do with the World Bank heist?"

"No comment," he managed to state just as he reached the door. He slipped inside, closed it behind him and breathed a sigh of relief.

Lennox was waiting for him, sitting in the outer office. The two had been working together almost nonstop since Jake had discovered his brother was missing, and Lennox hadn't once pressured Jake to get back to the job he was being paid to do—trace the missing money. He was a decent man.

"Your assistant's not coming in this morning," he said. "He arrived, saw that mob out there and kept right on driving. You weren't here yet when he called in to explain, but I told him I'd let you know."

"That's fine, there's no need for him to subject himself to this insanity. I thought we agreed to keep Zach's disappearance quiet. How did they find out?"

"Damned if I know. The media don't seem to have any details. Just that your brother is missing. It's all gossip right now. But I think we're going to have to make a statement soon."

"And tell them what? We don't know any more than they do."

"We know he didn't just go off on an unplanned vacation. We have the security tapes from the parking lot." He nodded toward the television that sat in the corner of the reception area, then picked up a remote control and pointed it.

The screen filled with the fuzzy outline of a parking lot. The tape was in black and white, and so out of focus, Jake couldn't tell one car from the next.

Lennox went to the screen, pointing at movement. "There. That's your brother's car. I think that's him inside it. Now see, another car pulls up behind his."

Jake leaned forward, his eyes narrowing on the unfocused blobs on the screen. The hazy shape that had to be Zach got out of his car and walked around to the hazy shape behind the wheel of the other car. He spoke to the driver for a moment, then went to the rear door and opened it.

A larger form walked up to Zach from behind, and then seemed to be helping Zach into the back seat of the second car.

"Wait, wait. Rewind that," Jake said, his eyes glued to the screen.

Lennox rewound, let it play again. The other person walked up to Zach, clapped a friendly arm around his shoulders. Zach's shape seemed stiff at first, then it relaxed, bending forward, and the person pushed or helped him into the back seat.

"This is ridiculous. You can't tell a damn thing from this tape."

"We're working on it. The FBI lab has a copy, and we've sent a second one to NASA. They'll use the same techniques they use to enhance satellite photos, see if they can clear this up any." He rewound, played it again. "You can see it better back at the lab, but note the way he goes stiff. At first I thought it was just surprise at this stranger walking up to him, but now I think it's more. I think they did something to him. See how he kinda jerks in reaction?"

"And then relaxes, lets that person put him right into the car, without a fight," Jake said. He watched the tape until the second car drove away, then he looked at Lennox. "You think they hurt him? Shot him, stabbed him, something like that?"

He shook his head. "Not a trace of blood or a hint that any shot was fired. No, I think it was something more subtle. A stun gun, maybe, though he'd have jerked around more. Could have been drugs.''

"Those bastards."

"The tape has a time stamp on it, Jake. At least we know exactly when he was taken. With any luck, the enhancement will give us a description of the car."

"Maybe even the plate number?" Jake asked.

"Let's hope."

He glanced toward the window, beyond which the reporters were still gathered. "What should we tell the press?"

"I think we have to confirm that Zach is missing, flash his face on the screen and tell them where he was last seen. The damage is done, Jake. This is gonna be all over the news before the day is out. We may as well use the public. Maybe someone saw something."

Jake nodded and started scribbling notes, while Lennox stepped outside to tell the press that Jake Ingram would have a statement for them within the hour. Then he went back inside, and the two wrote, erased and wrote some more, anguishing over just how much to reveal.

Finally Jake picked up the photo of himself and his brother, arm in arm, from his desk, removed it from its frame and gave Lennox a nod.

When he stepped outside, the reporters were more organized and quieter. They held microphones on long poles, and cameras whirred, aimed at his face.

"At approximately 4:00 p.m. on Wednesday evening, my brother, Professor Zachary Ingram, left his classroom at Greenlaurel University and walked to his car in the university parking lot. He never made it. The car remained in the lot until it was impounded by the authorities. It is possible that Zach left the university parking lot in the back of a second vehicle. If there is anyone who saw Zach in another car that evening, they should contact us. This is his photo."

He held up the photo. Cameras zoomed in on it.

"You look so much alike," someone shouted. "Which one is Zach?"

"Zach's on the left."

"Mr. Ingram, is there any chance this could be related to your involvement in the investigation of the World Bank heist?"

"We have no idea where my brother is, or why. But there is no evidence to suggest this is in any way related to the WBH."

More questions were shouted, but Jake held up his hands, shook his head. "I'm sorry, that's all we know. Please broadcast this photo as widely as you can. If anyone has seen my brother, please call the police and let them know."

Lennox stepped in front of Jake, taking over. "We've set up a tip line. If anyone has any information concerning the whereabouts of Zachary Ingram, they should call this number."

As Lennox spoke, Jake used the opportunity to slip back into the haven of his private office. But when he got there, he stopped in his tracks. There was a scent lingering in the air. A familiar scent that tugged at something in his mind, something long buried.

Violets.

He searched the place, seeing no one, no explanation for the smell—until he homed in on the envelope that rested on his desk.

It hadn't been there before, he was certain of that. He leaned closer, sniffed it and realized it was the source of the smell permeating the air now. It could be evidence, he knew. Of what, he couldn't begin to guess. Still, he used a pencil to hold it in place, and another to lift the unsealed flap of the envelope and then to wriggle the single sheet of velum out onto the desk. He used the same method to unfold the paper, and then quietly read the words that were written there in an elegant, spidery script, with the scent of violets setting off fireworks in his brain.

My darling Jake,

I must see you. I have information for you. It's high time you knew the truth about who you are, who you *really* are. Not the lies you've been told all your life, but at long last, the truth. You are special, Jake, and it's time for you to remember.

Meet me tonight, at midnight, on the footbridge that spans Rapid Creek at Greenlaurel State Park. Come alone. We'll both be in grave danger if anyone finds out I'm speaking to you. And be careful, my darling. Be very careful. It wasn't your brother they wanted, you know. It was you.

Love always,
V.

Lennox came back inside, and when Jake heard him, he refolded the paper, stuck it into the envelope and tucked it into his inside jacket pocket.

"That should keep them for a while," Lennox said as he took a seat. "I promised we'd give advance notice if any more information came to light, so— Hey, what's that smell?"

"Violets," Jake said. God, why did the word make his throat want to tighten as if with a rush of emotion? "Just some air freshener. I thought it was getting stale in here."

He ought to tell Lennox about the note. Send it off to the forensics lab for a complete analysis. He knew he ought to. And yet he didn't.

He was going to meet her, the woman who'd written this note and the last one. And he knew it was a woman, had no doubt of that, because of the contents of the letter, its innate gentleness, because of the feminine scrawl of the writing, and because of that scent. He could almost see her face. It hovered in his mind just beyond the fringes of perception. Just out of reach.

He knew the woman who smelled of violets. He *knew* her.

But how?

Lennox's voice broke his thoughts. "We're going to have to start thinking about security for you, Jake. Just in case this does turn out to be related. I know you're against the idea, but it's only logical. Especially now that word is out."

Jake nodded slowly. He'd insisted on protection for his fiancée, Tara, and the other members of his family. But so far, he'd steadfastly refused it for himself. And now, with tonight's mission in mind, he would have to refuse it just a little longer. "We'll discuss it tomorrow."

"Jake, I don't think—"

"Look, I can't even think about it now. I haven't even discussed any of this with Tara. Just give me until tomorrow, all right?"

He barked the words and knew he'd had no call to be so short with Lennox, but the other man sighed and nodded. "But tomorrow, we have to address this. Okay?"

Jake nodded. "Yeah. All right."

"Okay, so we have it clear, then?" Maisy asked Zach. She was nervous. Zach could tell she was nervous. He was so damn sick of lying in this bed he could have screamed the walls down. But it was worse seeing how tense and jittery she was, as they waited for Bob to return from the barn.

"I know what to do. As soon as he's back, I have some kind of convulsive fit. You report that I'm extremely ill and need to be hospitalized. He'll refuse or make up some excuse, and reluctantly you'll agree to keep me here one more day, insisting that you have to watch me every second."

She nodded, then searched his face. "Will it work, Zach?"

"It'll put him off," he said. "It won't *turn* him off." He was still angry that she had felt she had to put herself at risk this way in order to save him. Her behavior toward Bob had been like dangling bloody meat in front of a shark. The thug had caught the scent, and he wouldn't back off now. Not until he'd fed. Which would happen over Zach's dead body. "We have to get out of here," he told her, not for the first time. "Tonight."

Then he glanced out the window, and his face tightened. "Hell, maybe before tonight."

"What is it?" She hurried forward, leaning over to look outside. And Zach knew what she saw. Bob, lumbering toward the house, a newspaper tucked under his arm. "Where the hell did he get that paper?" she asked.

"It's either the one he stole from you, or a brand-new issue. And if it's a new one and I've been reported missing, we're in trouble."

"Once he knows you're not Jake— Oh, hell, Zach, what should I do?"

"Give me a second. Let me think—"

But before he finished speaking, she was heading for the door.

"What the hell are you doing?"

"Getting that newspaper away from him. He may not have had the chance to look at it yet." Then she was out of the room, hurrying along the hall, down the stairs, calling Bob's name in a sweet, sexy voice.

"Damn…"

Zach got out of bed and went to the door. His legs were still weak, and he was a little off balance, but far better than he'd been before. He had to get down there. He gripped the doorknob and turned it.

Locked. The damn thing was locked. And he was standing there, naked.

He hurried to the dresser where Bob had put the clothes he'd bought and pulled them on. Then he went through the bathroom, heading for Maisy's room.

"Well now," Bob said, grinning in a way that made her shiver, tossing his newspaper onto the table. "Eager little thing, aren't you?"

She stood a foot from him in the kitchen, and her fake smile faltered. But she glanced past him, to where the newspaper had landed on the table, and saw the headline splashed across the front page underneath a photograph of Zach and another man who looked enough like him to be his twin. "Professor Zachary Ingram Missing."

"Come here," Bob growled. He gripped her shoulders and hauled her closer, smashing her body to his, snapping his arms around her to hold her there. He still smelled of the barn as his hands closed on her backside, lifting her off her feet, turning her around and setting her on the kitchen table. She shifted her bottom to cover the newspaper.

"Bob, um, I don't think this is—"

"Oh, come on now. You've been teasing me all morning. Don't tell me you were only playing with me?"

"No, of course not. I just thought—"

"You know what? I don't really care what you think."

His voice had changed. Grown darker and more menacing.

"Bob? What are you talking about?"

He smiled slowly, shook his head as if he thought her an idiot. "Maisy, Maisy, Maisy. It's just you and me out here. Now, you led me to believe you wanted this as much as I did. But I really don't care whether you want it or not. It's not as if you have much of a choice in the matter."

Her blood seemed to turn to ice as he cupped her head and mashed his mouth to hers. She wrenched her hands from between their bodies, pressed her palms to his chest and pushed as hard as she could.

He drew away from her all of the sudden, so fast she didn't know what to think, and then his fist was coming at her face, and she had no time to duck.

The blow caught her in the temple and outer eye, knocking her sideways, right off the table onto the floor. Pain exploded in her head, and as she lay there, hurting, struggling to gather her senses and figure out what to do, he was kneeling over her, jerking her roughly from her side onto her back. Then he grabbed the front of her blouse and ripped it open.

"I knew you were just a tease. I knew it all along, Maisy. Playing me for an idiot. For a fool. But you asked for it, and you're damn well going to get it. No woman teases me and gets away with it."

She crossed her arms over her chest. He gripped them and forced them outward, pressed to the floor on either side of her. Then he bent over her breasts, like a hungry man at a feast.

In that instant something shattered over Bob's head, bits of pottery showering her face. Unaffected by the blow, Bob rose to his feet. He turned in time to take a punch in the face from Zach. But the bigger man barely even flinched.

Maisy scrambled off the floor, yanked a heavy frying pan from the stove and swung it for all she was worth.

It smashed against Bob's head, and he dropped to his knees with a howl of pain. Rising, he gripped a chair and hurled it at her. The blow sent her reeling, and she hit the door, shattering the glass with her head and sinking to the floor.

"Keep your hands off her!" she heard Zach shout.

Maisy watched in horror as Zach drove the large butcher knife into Bob's middle. Bob staggered backward, stunned, blood oozing from around the blade. Only half the length of the blade had sunk into his belly. Bob clenched the wooden handle with both hands, jerked it free and threw it in Maisy's direction. It missed her, but she didn't see where it landed.

Bob sank to his knees. Zach followed, kicked him in the head when he tried to get up. Bob went down one last time, and this time, he didn't get up again. Zach straddled the fallen man, pounding his face, right up until Maisy managed to call his name.

He stopped suddenly, staring down at the bloody face, then looking at his raw knuckled fists as if he didn't quite recognize them. Slowly he got off Bob, then turned, and rushed to where Maisy was struggling to get to her feet.

Her blouse was shredded, just her bra and jeans were in place, and her shoes, thank goodness, since the floor was covered in broken glass.

Zach picked her up, brushing the glass from her hair, and shoulders. He reached for the door handle.

She stopped him. "No, wait. Meat. There's meat in the fridge."

He set her down in a chair, opened the fridge and pulled out a package of steaks. "This?"

"Yes."

Zach set it on the table, then, glancing at Bob, who still lay on the floor, seemed to have another thought. He looked around the room, spotted a toaster, then grabbed a large knife from a drawer and sliced its power cord off. He did the same to the can opener, then stuck the knife into his waistband and knelt beside the fallen hulk, rolled him over and bound his hands behind his back, and legs at the ankles. Then he searched Bob's pockets, and pulled out a set of keys. "Yours?" he asked.

"Yes, those are my car keys. Are there any others?"

He finished his search. "No. His keys are either in the truck or hidden somewhere."

Nodding, Zach got up again and turned to scoop Maisy up as before. She grabbed the package of meat off the table as they passed. "Walk slowly, Zach. The dog—"

Even before she finished speaking, the beast came charging toward them.

Zach stilled, stiffened.

"Hello, Rufus, sweet boy," Maisy said. "Yes, you are. Come here. Come on, come here, boy."

The dog slowed its pace, stopped snarling. It cocked its ears and tipped its head to one side.

"Look what I have for you, boy," she said, ripping the plastic wrap open, fishing out a piece of steak and holding it in front of her. "See? You want this, hmm?"

The dog's tail began to wag, and it trotted closer. When it got close enough, Maisy dropped the meat and the dog caught it before it hit the ground.

"The car," she whispered. "We have to try to get to the car."

Zach carried her to the car, and the dog followed, no longer growling. At the side of the car, Zach set her down on her feet. "Are you all right?"

She closed her eyes and knew damn well she

wasn't all right. Far from it. She couldn't seem to stand up on her own, and had to lean on the car for support. "I'll be fine. You check the car I'll keep the dog distracted."

Nodding, Zach hurried to the driver's door, popped the hood and glanced underneath. Then he lay on the ground and slid under the car to inspect the bottom.

He slid out again. "He's rigged it with what looks like explosives, Doc."

Maisy stilled, with a piece of meat dangling from her fingers. "What?"

"It doesn't look like he ever intended for you to survive long enough to get back home."

It shook her to the core. "My God."

"His truck is right there."

The dog leaped upward, snatching the meat from her numb fingers, nearly getting them as well. Zach went to the truck and looked inside. "No keys. And it's got a Club. Can you believe that? A Club."

"Wait," Maisy said as he stood there with the truck door open. She swung her hand, and a slice of raw meat arched through the air, and landed neatly on the seat of the truck. The dog followed a split second later, and Zach closed the pickup's door.

Then he bent to jab his knife into all four of its tires, one by one. He stuck the knife back into his waistband, returned to Maisy and scooped her up again.

"I can walk," she protested.

"Your head's split open, your pupils are as big as planets and you're swaying on your feet. Which way is the barn?"

She pointed, and he carried her.

Eleven

Zach had never beaten anyone up before, much less plunged a blade into someone's belly. It amazed and sickened him that his rage against Bob had carried him to such a dark place. A place where he could have beaten the man to death, had the doc's soft plea not snapped him out of it. Or maybe he had beaten and stabbed Bob to death. The thought made Zach ill, but he was fairly certain Bob had been dancing along the honed edge of the Reaper's blade.

Zach had never been that out of control before.

But when he'd seen the man assaulting Maisy—mauling her, hitting her—something primal came roaring to life inside him. A part of him he barely recognized.

Now she was hurt, no longer the rescuer. It was up to him to save them both. He hoped to God he was up to the task.

He set Maisy in the barn and, guided by her pained voice, opened the back door and took a scoop of grain out to the pasture, where she said the horses were. As soon as they caught a whiff of the grain, they followed him back into the barn. He closed the back door and turned to Maisy, who sat on a bale of hay. "Are there saddles, bridles?"

"No. Nothing."

He looked around. "Okay. I guess we have to manage with what's at hand." He located some loose baling twine.

"Take Spike and Dusty," she said. She was holding what had been a part of her sleeve to the cut on her head. "Diamond is going to foal any day now and Blizzard is too old."

He blinked, cocking his head at her.

"The red one and the gray one, Zach. Take the red one and the gray one."

Nodding, he returned to the horses, seeing why she'd chosen the names she had. Spike had a short mane that stuck straight up between his ears, and Dusty was the gray color of dust. Zach sliced off lengths of the twine and fastened them to the horses' halters to use as makeshift reins, hoping it would work. He made some longer lengths, by tying numerous strands together, to use as lead ropes. Then he let the other two horses out the back door, closed it behind them and led Dusty and Spike out the front door. Since Dusty was bigger, he was the one Zach chose to ride.

"Come on, sweetie. Got to get up now." He scooped Maisy up and set her on Dusty's back. Then he tied one of the long leads to Spike's halter and, holding the end of it, climbed on behind the doc.

She leaned back against him, and he kicked the

horse's sides, steering it in what he sincerely hoped was the right direction, leading the other horse behind.

"Stay off the roads, Zach. Stick to the fields. If you can get to the woods, that would be even better. We can't let them find us."

He nodded, holding her against him with one arm, still quivering with rage at what that bastard had done to her.

And then a sound blasted the air, and something whizzed past his ear.

Zach looked behind them and saw Bob in the distance, pointing a rifle. "Jesus, the bastard's still alive. And there's another vehicle in the driveway!"

He kicked the horse's sides and held Maisy against him as it sprang into a full, teeth-jarring gallop.

Maisy was drifting, barely clinging to consciousness, and not quite clear whether the thoughts and memories drifting through her mind were things she was dreaming or things she was saying aloud.

She remembered Michael coming home, looking distraught. Remembered how he hadn't been sleeping well, and how she had known something was terribly wrong, but had been completely taken by surprise when he told her just what it was.

He said he was in over his head. He said he'd made a terrible mistake and couldn't get out of it, and didn't know what to do. He begged me to understand, told me he needed me more than he ever had. And then he told me he'd been sleeping with one of his patients.

Soft hands stroked Maisy's hair. Someone whispered, "It's okay, Doc. It's all in the past."

But it's not in the past. Not really. It's with me, all the time. It's the reason I took refuge behind the wall of my work. I research and I write about it. When I lecture, I'm at a podium, removed from everyone else, above them with this clear line of demarcation between myself and everyone else. I consult, I oversee the psychiatric teams doing the hands-on work with the patients in need of deprogramming. I don't get involved. I don't work one-on-one with patients.

"He broke your heart, and you've been hiding it ever since."

She sighed, feeling warmth all around her, pressing herself nearer to that warmth as her thoughts flowed more freely than they ever had before.

It wasn't his fault. What we had, Michael and I, was nice. Comfortable. We were compatible and we were close. But there was never a fiery passion between us, never the kind of madness she felt for him. He went back to her that night, because I told him it was the right thing to do. They went for a drive and he explained to her, clearly and rationally, why he had to end his relationship with her. At least, that was the plan. I had no grasp of what that woman was feeling for him, no experience with emotions that powerful.

She felt tears rolling down her cheeks. She hadn't felt tears in a very long time.

The police said it was an accident, but I knew it wasn't. I read his journals after he died. He wrote that the woman's passion for him was overwhelming, frightening. He said he was afraid she'd kill them both if he tried to end it. But he tried, anyway. Because I told him it was the right thing to do. And she did it. She killed them both.

"She killed them both," she heard herself saying. And she suddenly wondered if she'd spoken all her thoughts aloud.

As her head slowly grew clearer, she found herself lying on the ground, surrounded by dense woods and darkness. The sounds that reached her, one by one, were numerous: water bubbling and rushing, birds singing, wind whispering through the branches overhead, a horse nickering. Her lower extremities were on the ground, but her upper body was cradled against a man's chest, surrounded by his arms. Her head was pillowed by his shoulder. He was stroking her hair.

"Zach?"

"Yeah, Doc. I'm right here. I've got you."

She sighed in relief, even as she felt a flash of alarm at being held so intimately against him. "Where are we?"

"We took the horses and ran, remember?" He sighed. "Bob was shooting at us. Someone else arrived, maybe Agnes and Oliver. I don't know. But they got him loose fast. I thought I'd killed him. I wish I had.''

She shook her head as the memories came back to her. Bob's assault, his attack, and Zach's rage when he'd walked in on it. He'd been furious, vicious and brutal.

"You're not the kind of man who could just kill someone," she said.

"I didn't used to think I was. But when I saw what he was doing to you, everything in me became that kind of man.'' He lowered his head, tipping her chin up with his fingers and searching her eyes. "That's what you're afraid of, isn't it? Not the whole silly doctor-patient nonsense you've been spouting. That's invalid and you know it. And it's not fear of being hurt again, either. At least not entirely. It's the passion. You feel it as much as I do, and you've seen what it can do. What it did to Michael and Kelly. It scares the hell out of you.''

She closed her eyes, because his were probing so deeply and seeing so much she couldn't bear it. "I've been talking a lot, haven't I?"

"Yeah. A lot."

"What else did I tell you?"

"You don't remember?"

She shook her head slowly.

"Then it doesn't matter. For what it's worth, Doc, this is hitting me like a ton of bricks, too. I'm a mild-mannered economics professor. I do not make a habit of beating up men twice my size, stealing horses or riding hell-bent-for-leather with a half-conscious beauty in my arms.''

She felt warm all over, and every cell in her body was alive and tingling and telling her to run from this feeling. Instead, she dared open her eyes again, peering into his. ''You did all that pretty well, for your first time.''

He smiled at her. ''To tell you the truth, it's kind of gratifying. I never thought of myself as the kind of man who could do any of that stuff. And for the past few days I've been helpless and weak and you've been playing the hero. That's tough on a man's ego.''

She lowered her eyes. ''Maybe…maybe that's all it is.''

''That's all what is?''

''You said yourself this isn't a normal set of circumstances—not for either of us. We've both been thrown into this tense, dangerous, life-and-death situation. It's no wonder everything seems heightened.''

''So you're saying that we aren't really as powerfully attracted to each other as we think we are. That it's just the situation making us feel this way?''

Relieved that he got her point, she closed her eyes and nodded. ''Yes.''

''No.''

''What?'' Her eyes opened again.

He didn't answer her. Instead, he cupped her cheek in his hand and kissed her. His mouth covered hers, nudging and urging until she parted her lips and kissed him back. Her heart pounded, her blood heated and he kept on kissing her. When his tongue touched her lips, she shivered, curling her arms around his neck and pressing closer to his body. He responded by holding her tighter.

When they pulled apart, they were both breathless. She blinked at him, and he stared into her eyes with fire burning in his.

"I don't think it's the situation," he told her. "I think it's considerably more than that. But I don't suppose we'll ever know for sure, until we're safe in our normal lives again. But I'll tell you something, Doc. I hope it feels the same then, because I want this kind of passion in my life."

She ignored her body's hungry insistence and whispered, "But I don't."

"How can you know that, if you've never had it?"

She shrugged. "How can you?"

He held her gaze, and she felt the answer to her question, even though he didn't say it aloud. How could either of them know they wanted this, unless they took it further? Maybe they should make love, right here on the forest floor, and see what unexplored levels this passion might have in store for them.

Her tummy tightened at the thought, and her body melted and softened and yearned. And yet her lips trembled and her heart beat as if a hummingbird were trapped inside it.

"I'm not ready for this, Zach," she whispered.

He closed his eyes slowly. "I wouldn't take advantage of you in this condition, or in this situation,

Doc. You've been through hell today, and you're hurting to boot. No. I wasn't suggesting anything.''

He wasn't?

He smiled. ''I might have been thinking it, but I wasn't suggesting it. Not right this minute, at least.''

''Oh.'' Somehow that made her feel better. She shivered a little and sat up, regretting the loss of his warmth, but knowing that if she didn't put some physical space between them, they'd start kissing again. Because she wanted to start kissing him again. And she didn't want to stop. She looked around and rubbed her arms against the chill.

''We can't really have a fire,'' he said. ''Even if I could manage to start one without a match. I'm not sure how far from the ranch we managed to get, but I don't want to give us away.''

''Maybe we should keep riding,'' she suggested.

''I thought the horses needed a rest. And you were…you were scaring me, to tell you the truth. I thought it best I let you lie still awhile.''

''Scaring you how?''

He shook his head. ''You took a blow to the head. Muttering unintelligibly is probably just a side effect.''

She nodded, noting the tightness around her head, reaching up to touch the strip of cloth he'd tied there. It was wet. Cold. He must have wet it in an icy stream, to get the swelling down, and tied it tight to stop the bleeding. ''How long has it been since we stopped?''

"A couple of hours." He looked at the horses, which were tied to a spot where at least some grass grew and where they could reach the water. "We can probably take off again, if you want."

"I think we should. Bob has help now, and they'll come looking."

Zach nodded, getting to his feet and reaching down to help her to hers. "Are you sure you're up to riding?"

"I'll be fine. Put me on Spike. We'll wear Dusty out if we keep riding double."

"Are you sure?"

At her nod he sighed. "Hell, I'm glad you're feeling better, but I'll miss having you in my arms."

She looked away, unsure what to say. Zach cleared his throat. "All right, then, here we go." Sliding an arm around her waist to steady her, he walked with her to where the horses stood. Then he turned toward her, bent a little, and picked her up in his arms, to set her on the back of Spike.

"Not letting this hero-cowboy thing go to your head, are you, Zach?"

He smiled at her. "Damn straight I am. Who knows when I'll get the chance again?" He handed her the reins. "Now if I only had a keen sense of direction or a clue where the hell we should be going…"

"Anywhere," she said. "As long as it's away from Bob and that ranch. As soon as we spot civilization, we can leave the horses hidden, sneak in on foot and use a phone to call for help."

"You're always ready with a plan, aren't you?"

"I try to be."

"Not much into spontaneity, then?"

She lowered her eyes. "Spontaneity usually comes with risk attached. I don't like risk."

"I didn't used to think I did, either," he said, getting onto his horse, taking up the reins and wheeling it around.

"And now?" she asked as her mount fell into step beside his.

"Now?" He lifted his brows, heaved a sigh. "You're a risk, Doc. This thing you're trying to pretend isn't real between us, that's a risk, too. I gotta tell you, risk is starting to look awful damn good to me."

If he were a risk, then inwardly Maisy knew it was looking pretty good to her as well. But she was scared. She was more afraid than she'd ever been in her life. And not of Bob and whoever else might be after them.

It had devastated her to lose Mike and her safe, comfortable marriage. But what she had felt for him hadn't begun to compare to the feelings surging inside her for Zach, this man she'd known for only a handful of days—but felt as if she'd known all her life.

She burned for him with a fire that threatened to consume her. And that frightened her more than Bob ever could.

As night fell, they rode, the doc falling in behind him, following where he led, as if he had a clue what the hell he was doing. He didn't know where they were or which way to go. He was basically following what appeared to be well-worn animal paths through the woods, and growing more tired with every hour that passed.

"My thought is to get us as far from Bob as possible, while keeping us in dense cover for as long as we can. At least for tonight," he said, trying the plan out on her, hoping it didn't sound as lame as he feared it might.

"I was thinking the same thing," she said.

"You were?"

"Yeah. Eventually, we're going to have to stop, get some sleep. I'll feel much safer doing that if we're deep in the forest."

He swallowed hard, nodding, pleased that they were thinking along the same lines. "The ground is pretty hard here. I don't think the horses are leaving any tracks."

"Just the occasional fragrant ones."

He glanced back at her with a smile. "Not much we can do about that."

"Let's hope they're not even following."

"We can't count on that, though."

"I know."

They rode on, along a twisting path that forked often, always choosing the branch that looked less traveled. Every once in a while, where the trees were older and the woods not as dense, he led them off the trail entirely, and they picked their way slowly through the forest, until they found another. It wouldn't be easy to track them, he thought. He hoped not, at least.

They were heading uphill. He wasn't sure why, but he felt instinctively that they should climb as high as possible, and Maisy wasn't objecting, so he assumed she didn't disagree. Eventually, he spotted a dark blotch in a steep section of the hillside ahead, visible in a pool of moonlight spilling down from above.

"Is that…?"

"A cave?" She finished his thought for him, sending an odd feeling trickling through his torso. God, it was as if they were communicating on some level beyond words. And it felt good, and right.

"Let's take a closer look," he said.

They rode nearer, stopping at a stream that gurgled across their path. The horses immediately bent their heads to drink.

"Let them have a rest, Zach. I'll stay with them."

"All right." He dismounted, and so did she, taking the baling twine reins of both horses and holding them while they drank. Zach looked around and listened intently for any suspicious sounds. But the only noises were natural ones. Night birds and the wind in the trees. "Yell if you need me."

"That would have me yelling from now until you get back," she told him.

The words made his chest tighten up. She wasn't flirting. She was sincere, and it touched him in a way that he hadn't been touched before. "I'll be quick," he promised. And he hurried to hop over the tiny stream and pick his way up the face of the hill, more slowly than he would have liked. It was steep, and footholds were tough to find in the dark, despite the moonlight. But eventually he made his way up to what was obviously a cave.

He stepped inside, wishing for a light. They'd planned to slip away from the ranch during the night, after surreptitiously gathering supplies throughout the day—matches, water, food, blankets.

As it was, they'd been forced out well ahead of schedule, and now they were facing the wilderness with nothing but themselves and a pair of stolen horses.

He gave his eyes a moment to adjust to the darkness, then walked farther into the cave, exploring its walls with his hands. He didn't find an exit or an ending. The cave was a deep one. Deeper than they needed. But there was no way they could get the horses inside.

Moving back to the entrance, he looked down, about twenty feet to where the doc waited with the two animals, which had apparently had their fill of water and were now nibbling at the grass. From this vantage point, Zach could see a good distance around them. They'd see even more by daylight, he would bet. This was good—a good spot. And a few yards behind Maisy, just past a very dense stand of pine trees, was a tiny clearing perfect for the horses.

He scrambled back down the slope, almost slipping when he stepped on a wet stone, but catching himself and then moving on, finally reaching the bottom and hurrying back to the doc.

"We were right, it is a cave. A nice deep one. We should spend the night here, sheltered from the wind."

She nodded. "The horses?"

"There's a nice view from up there. I think I spotted the perfect place for them. Follow me." He took Dusty's reins from her and led the horse forward. She came behind, leading Spike, as Zach sought a way through the wall of pines. When he came to a break between interlocking branches, he led the horse through.

Maisy came behind him. "Oh, this is great," she told him. "I was wondering what we'd do with the horses for the night."

"The trees really hide it well." From his pockets he yanked the lead ropes he'd made of twine and attached one to each horse's harness, removing the makeshift reins to avoid the animals getting tangled. Then he tied the leads to limbs that had some give to them, allowing the horses even more room to move about. He made sure they could reach the little stream that trickled through the clearing.

When he finished, he saw that the doc was nodding in approval.

"You think they'll be all right for the night?" he asked.

She kept on nodding. "I think they'll be fine. We haven't worked them too hard." She moved closer to Dusty, running her hands over his coat. "They aren't sweaty, and it's not that cold out. I think they'll be great." She patted the horse's rump, looking at Zach now. "You're good at this."

"I'm guessing, at best."

"Then you're a good guesser."

"How can you be so sure?"

"We're out here, free, not locked up in some farmhouse and guarded by a sex-starved slug." She tipped her head to one side. "You must be doing something right."

He hoped he was doing something right. He reached a hand to her, and she took it, letting him lead her back out through the pines, across the little stream, to the face of the hill. Then he let go of her hand.

"You go first. That way if you stumble I'll be right behind you. The footholds are tough to find, but they're there. Go slow, feel your way and take your time."

She nodded and began the climb. He told her where to find footholds, when he remembered. More often he didn't, but he climbed right behind her, ready to grab her if she fell.

The rock face grew steeper, and her grip faltered when she reached for the rock where he'd stumbled earlier. She slid down and he shot his hands upward, cupping her buttocks and holding her steady. "Sorry.

I should have warned you," he said, still holding her. "It's wet right there."

"Yeah, it sure is." She reached out up again. "I think it's a spring, Zach. The water seems to be coming right out of the rocks." He watched as she brought her cupped hand to her mouth and sipped the water. Then she repeated the action several more times. "It's good, sweet and cold."

"That's a relief. I'm as thirsty as those horses were." He didn't mention that holding her butt in his hands like this seemed to be making his throat drier by the second.

She continued upward, climbing higher, ending up on the ledge just outside the cave opening. He moved up to the spring, spent a moment drinking his fill, then joined her there.

"This is pretty creepy, Zach," she said, peering into the darkness. "Do you think there could be anything in there?"

"I don't think this is bear country, Doc."

She glanced sideways at him. "I don't think so, either. But there are plenty of cougars."

He hadn't thought of that. "I wandered a good ways back in the darkness," he said with a shrug. "Nothing ate me."

"Well, that's a good sign." She moved forward beyond the reach of the milky moon glow. "All the same, I think this is as far as I want to venture."

"It's fine. We're sheltered, and not in view from outside." He sat down, putting his back to the cool stone wall. She did the same, sitting close beside him. "I wish we could start a fire, cook some food. Even a blanket would be nice. I'm sorry I didn't think to grab anything before we left the house."

She laid her hand gently on his shoulder. "I think we both know what Bob had in mind for me," she said softly. "You saved me from that. And maybe worse."

Zach put an arm around her, pulling her closer, and she leaned her head on his shoulder. "When it gets light outside, we might be able to get our bearings, figure out where to go."

"Do you think they even bothered coming after us?" she asked.

Zach nodded. "I think by now word must have gotten out that I've disappeared. My brother and I talk just about every day. He had to know something was wrong." He drew a deep breath. "If the press got wind that Jake Ingram's brother was missing, it would have been big news, because of Jake's involvement with the World Bank heist investigation. Agnes and Oliver had to have heard about it. If that was them—"

"It doesn't matter. Bob would know by now, anyway. It was splashed across the front page of that newspaper he was carrying back from the barn." Maisy shivered and burrowed closer. "They wouldn't have just let you go, would they, Zach?"

"No more than they intended to let you go, judging by the explosives rigged to your car."

"They would have killed us both, and then probably gone after your brother."

"Yeah. And if I don't get to a phone so I can warn Jake pretty soon, I'm afraid they might get to him first."

She looked up at him. "I hadn't even thought of that. My God, Zach, you must be worried to death."

"I am. But Jake's tough. And he's not stupid enough to just walk into a trap. Especially if he knows what's happened to me. His guard will be up."

"Let's hope so."

"That's all we *can* do right now, Doc. That, and try to get a little sleep, so we can do what we need to do tomorrow."

She nodded. Zach shifted lower until he was lying flat on the hard floor of the cave, and Maisy lay curled in his arms, close to his side. He held her tight, and told himself that he was going to behave the way his upbringing dictated, the way his values dictated. The fires she had kindled inside him suggested otherwise.

Twelve

Jake waited in the darkness on the bridge, where the note had told him to meet the mysterious author of the violet-scented letter. It was a footbridge, small, wooden, arching, set halfway along a three-mile path at Greenlaurel State Park. He'd left his car in the parking area at the trailhead, a mile and a half back. There was no lighting out here, and at this hour, not another soul to be seen. There had been no other vehicles in the parking area, and he was beginning to wonder just how stupid it was for him to come out here alone.

He liked to think he could handle himself if the worst happened. Just as a precaution, though, he pulled his cell phone from his pocket, pressed a button and looked at its illuminated face.

No Service.

The words didn't change, even when he extended the antenna and moved the phone in different directions. He should have figured there'd be no reception out here in the forest.

Something moved behind him, and he spun around, then froze, watching, waiting. Moonlight spilled from the sky, but the moon was high and distant. The pale glow didn't allow him to see very far, the entire trail snug beneath a canopy of trees.

Again he heard the sounds. A couple of footsteps. Rustling branches.

He wondered if maybe he should have brought a gun with him.

The steps came again—two quick, one slower. He heard the distinct sound of breathing. Almost... sniffing. Another step, and another. Slowly, a form took shape in the darkness.

There was a snort, a stomp, and then the deer whirled and leaped off into the forest.

Jake felt his coiled muscles relax as the breath he hadn't realized he'd been holding escaped all at once. He even smiled a little at his own nervousness. A deer. It was only a freaking deer.

Which begged the question, where was the woman who was supposed to meet him here? He glanced at his watch, wishing he'd bought the one with the luminous dial, and tried angling it into the moonlight enough to read the time.

She should have been here twenty minutes ago. But maybe she was waiting, watching him, just making sure he had come alone as he'd promised. It was risky, coming out here like this—he knew that. Especially since he'd told no one about the note or the meeting.

But if it had something to do with his brother's abduction, he was more than willing to take the risk. Just as he was more than willing to risk anything else, including Tara's anger. And God, she was angry. Furious, when he'd told her their wedding date might have to be postponed again. He'd hoped that the news of his brother's disappearance would have softened her reaction, made her understand just how much pressure Jake was under right now. But it hadn't.

He didn't suppose he could blame her. It wasn't the first time he'd had to change the wedding date. But the entire world was looking to him to solve this crime. If he failed, there could be complete economic collapse. Add to that the fact that his beloved brother was missing, and something had to give.

The wedding was the only thing that could.

Tara believed that was because it was at the bottom of Jake's list of priorities. But given the load resting on his shoulders right now, he didn't see how it could be pushed any higher.

Sighing, he leaned against the footbridge's rail, resigned to wait there for as long as it took.

Maisy slept, she wasn't certain for how long, but she did sleep. She must have, because she didn't remember twining herself around Zach, but that was obviously what she had done. They lay on their sides, facing each other. Her thigh lay over his, her calf curving under his. Her hips and his were pressed together, and there was a hardness there that told her he probably wasn't asleep anymore, either.

She'd wrapped one arm around his waist, and her

other arm pillowed his head. And when she opened her eyes she found him staring into them.

Neither of them moved. She didn't dare stir. And yet it was so intimate, the way they lay, she knew she should back away.

She didn't.

"Maisy?" he whispered.

"Yes."

"If I don't kiss you right now, I'm going to go up in flames."

"Yes."

He pressed his mouth to hers. She kissed him back.

It wasn't tender, this kiss. It wasn't tentative and it wasn't gentle. It was hungry, seeking, probing, tasting. He stroked her mouth with his tongue, and she tangled her fingers in his hair. When he started moving his hips against her, she responded in kind, arching against him, telling him with her body that she was tired of fighting this attraction. She wanted him.

He wriggled a hand between them, tugging the knotted shirttails of her torn blouse, and then pushed the fabric apart. She rolled onto her back to help him, and he rose above her, straddling her, opening the blouse wide. Then his hands found her breasts in the darkness, fumbled with the front hook of her bra, freed it and peeled it away. And at last his palms rubbed over her bare flesh, skimming her nipples. He closed his fingers on them, rolling and pulling as they hardened in response.

"It's too damn dark. I wish I could see you."

She was glad of the darkness, but she didn't say so. She wouldn't have had time to say much of anything, anyway, because he bent his head and caught her breast in his mouth, sucking and nibbling, taking her breath away.

Her hands clasped his head to her as he fed on the nipple. He slid his other hand down her belly, to the jeans, then unfastened them and slid his hand inside, inside her panties and lower. His fingers parted her and explored, probing, entering, rubbing. He found the pulsing core of her need and used his thumb to tease and torment it, while his fingers pressed against her, sliding in and out until she was shivering and wet.

She reached up to him, trembling as she unbuttoned his shirt and ran her hands over his naked chest, then lower, to unfasten his jeans. She shoved them down over his hips, shorts and all. And then, emboldened by his merciless stroking, and by the darkness, she closed her hand around his erection. It was silky smooth, ridged and hard, warm. She squeezed and stroked it, her thumb moving over the tip, and he shuddered.

He took his hand away just long enough to slide her jeans and panties off. He kicked his own clothing free, and she peeled the rest of hers off and lay there, naked, chilled and burning up at once.

And then he came to her again, his hands parting her legs, then sliding up along her waist to her breasts as he lowered himself atop her. She felt him pressing against her, and then inside her, deeper, and still deeper.

"It's been…a long time for me," she whispered.

"It won't be again." He pushed himself deeper yet, filling her completely, and she gripped his shoulders hard as he began to move. Then she was moving, too, moving with him, meeting him. His hands slid beneath her to cup her buttocks, arching her up to take more of him. His thighs pressed hers wider, opening her up so he could push even deeper. She felt possessed, as if she no longer had control of her body. The feelings flooding it, the fire burning it, the tremors racking it—even the sounds she made were not of her own volition, but being driven from her throat by the man inside her. It was as if she were an instrument he'd decided to play. And he knew how. God, he knew how. He knew when to kiss her and lick her mouth. He knew when to take her breast, when to suckle, when to bite. He knew just how hard to squeeze her bottom, and how to tug it to him a little harder, and then harder still, so he could bury himself inside her to the hilt.

And he knew when she'd reached the edge, and proceeded to push her over. She cried his name over and over as the pulsing orgasm held her in its grip. It went on and on, and then he was shuddering and gasping, and withdrawing completely from her.

She nearly protested, nearly gripped him and held him to her, but as the waves of pleasure faded, she understood. He was protecting her. He sank to the floor beside her, and she rolled into his arms, holding him, stroking his wonderful shoulders and back.

"Thank you for that," she whispered.

His arms came around her waist. "No, baby. Thank *you.*" He held her closer, nuzzling her hair, kissing her forehead.

"Zach, I..."

"Hmm?"

"I...don't want...I'm not ready for..."

He drew back slightly, looking down at her face even though he couldn't really see it in the darkness of the cave. "You're not ready for what? A relationship with me?"

"With anyone. This has all happened so fast, and I just— I need time."

He sighed deeply, then remained silent for a long moment. Finally he said, "So I should think of this as just casual sex?"

The words pricked her, and she stiffened. "I don't have casual sex. For three years I haven't had any sex at all."

"I'm sorry, I shouldn't have said that. I know you don't take sex lightly. Neither do I. And I knew you weren't ready. I should have never—"

"No." She pressed a finger to his lips. "No, Zach, don't get me wrong. I don't regret what happened between us just now. I wanted it as much as you did. It's...it's what comes next that worries me."

His hand stroked over her hair. "You mean, like,

my pulling you into my arms and making love to you again?" He leaned close, kissed her lips.

She kissed him back, and when he stopped for air, she whispered, "No. I'm not afraid of that. I want that."

"Then you're worried about things like what we're going to be to each other."

"Yes, exactly. What we plan, where we go. What happens when we get back to our boring, real-world lives and find that all this passion has evaporated."

"That's not going to happen, Maisy. And as to what we're going to be to each other—what we maybe already are to each other—I hate to break it to you, but I don't think we have a hell of a lot of say about that."

She lowered her head, resting it against his shoulder. His strong, safe, comforting shoulder. She kissed him there. "Maybe not. But right now we can only focus on getting ourselves out of this mess alive, and warning your brother. Anything else just has to wait. I can't deal with it, not now."

"You're scared," he told her. "Hell, I don't blame you. I'm scared of this thing, too. But I know it's not all in my head." He paused, sighed, then leaned closer to kiss her cheek. "I suppose if I'd been betrayed the way you were, though, I might be a little more wary. I understand, Doc. And I trust in this thing enough to wait until you're ready to do the same."

"Really?"

"Yeah. Really. And if you want to cuddle up and

go to sleep, I'll hold you all night and not ask for anything more.''

She pressed a gentle kiss to his lips. "I'm not quite ready to go to sleep just yet.''

Daylight came. During the night they'd stirred awake once more, when their heated bodies had cooled enough to feel the chill in the air. They'd dressed and snuggled together for a couple more hours, and the doc had gone back to sleep.

Zach hadn't. He'd lain there holding her in his arms, wondering what lay ahead for the two of them. Whether they would survive this trek through the wilderness or become hopelessly lost and die of exposure or starvation or thirst. Whether their enemies would track them down and kill them in a far more efficient way.

It was almost as scary to think about what came next for them if they did survive. Would Maisy Dalton's fear of betrayal keep her from embracing the feelings that he felt growing between them? He stared down at her, watching her sleep, almost willing her to trust him. It was going to take some effort to heal her wounds, to win her trust. And once he had won it, he'd better make damn sure he never broke it. Tough as she was with kidnappers and would-be rapists, he didn't think she was strong enough to take another heartbreak.

Maybe she was right to be cautious. Maybe he needed to slow down a little himself, make absolutely sure his feelings were genuine and that they would last, before pushing her too hard.

Although after last night...

He closed his eyes and tried to quell the rising tide of emotions and longing inside him. The mere memory of her—her arms around him, her body holding him—was enough to send his blood pressure soaring. It was going to be hard to take it slow after that. It was going to be damn near impossible.

He opened his eyes again and focused on the horizon outside the cave, which was paler now than it had been before. And as he lay there, holding her, watching, it grew lighter still, and then the upper curve of a fiery sun rose lazily, turning the sky into a rainbow of vivid colors. A few fingerlike clouds floated past, and turned purple, pink and yellow at the touch of the sun's light.

"Doc," he whispered, bending to speak close to her ear.

"Mmm?"

"Roll over. You've gotta see this."

She blinked her eyes open, frowning up at him, then rolled over to see what was so interesting. "Oh." The word was little more than a breath, and full of awe.

His arms linked around her waist, holding her close as the two of them watched the sun come up. It was so breathtaking that he almost forgot the hunger gnawing at his belly for those few minutes.

But when the sun had completed its morning display and hung in the sky, beaming heat and warmth and white light into the cave, he knew they had to get moving. Reluctantly, he took his arms from around Maisy, and got to his feet. "You must be starving," he said.

"You, too."

"Ravenous." When her eyes shot to his, he knew she was looking for a double entendre. She probably found it, because he caught fire whenever her eyes met his. But he'd promised not to push her. "I could eat a horse," he added.

"Well, horse we have." She smiled a little at her own joke. "I wonder if we're anywhere near civilization?"

He walked to the cave's opening, and she got up and came behind him. He could see nothing. Just trees and more trees. Then he turned to look behind and above. The cave was set midway up a good size hill. "Maybe if I climbed to the top..."

"It doesn't look safe, Zach."

"Then I'll have to be careful. Why don't you go on down and check on the horses while I head up and see what I can see?"

She wanted to argue, he could tell. But he also knew that it was useless to continue wandering aimlessly through the forest with no clue where they were going. If he could just get his bearings...

She gave in with a sigh and a nod, then slowly made her way down the hillside, pausing for a drink at the spring. He watched her until she got to the bottom, and then she stood there, looking back up at him. Clearly she had no intention of going through that wall of pines to check on the animals until she saw that he'd made it to the top.

He edged out onto the cave's ledge, found the shallowest approach and began climbing upward, moving carefully. Every now and then he would think he'd gone as far as he could, with no more footholds or handholds within reach, but every time that happened he managed to find one if he just kept trying.

Gradually, he made his way to the top, where he straightened, looking down to where Maisy was still waiting. She stood there, far below, and waved at him. He waved back, then turned to take a look around.

His heart sank when he didn't see any church steeple or barn roof in the distance. But there was a path—actually, it looked more like a road. Not a paved one, perhaps a log road used by loggers who periodically thinned the timber in these forests. Or maybe a fire trail. In state forests, it was common to see sporadic breaks, wide lanes with nothing but grass, which were kept cleared in case of forest fires.

Either way, the traveling would be easy, and the trail would lead to the outermost edge of the forest. But wait—there was something there, on the trail.

A vehicle. A green SUV.

It was the same vehicle he'd seen in the driveway as they'd fled from the ranch!

He whirled to look down at Maisy, but she was no longer there. And then he scrambled down the hillside as quickly as he could manage, to warn her that their enemies were near.

Maisy was nowhere in sight at the bottom. She'd apparently seen that he was going to make it down in one piece, and had gone ahead to check on the horses.

He walked toward the wall of pines and picked his way through them, emerging on the other side. He looked ahead, found her, and then froze—because there was a gun pressed to her temple.

Bob stood behind her holding the gun, his other arm wrapped around her, pinning her arms to her sides and her body to the front of his.

Zach swallowed the rush of fear, anger and rage that rose inside him. "You surprised me, Bob. I didn't think you were bright enough to track us on your own."

"He wasn't," said a female voice.

Zach jerked his head to the left, only to see Agnes coming toward him, a gun in her hand as well. And when he looked to the right, he saw Oliver, also holding a gun, but looking decidedly uncomfortable about doing so.

"It's good to see you again, Mr. Ingram," Agnes said. "Mr. *Zachary* Ingram, isn't it?"

He turned his attention back to her, knowing instinctively she was a far more serious threat than either of the men. She had a newspaper in her free hand, the one that wasn't pointing a weapon at him, and she held it up. "It's all over the news. Zachary Ingram, brother of famed economist Jake Ingram, missing. Police suspect foul play."

"Then it *is* my brother you're after," Zach said. "Why?"

She smiled slowly. "I could tell you that, Mr. Ingram, but then I'd have to kill you." She tipped her head to one side. "Then again, I have to kill you anyway. But I'm still not going to tell you. You've been far too much trouble to me already. Do you have any idea how busy I am?"

Zach shrugged. "Guess you should have hired better help."

"This, unfortunately, is all too true," Agnes said, with a disgusted glance in Bob's direction. "For God's sake, stop fondling the woman and bind her. We don't have all day."

Zach shot Bob a murderous look, and it wasn't forced or make-believe. The man's hand had been closed on Maisy's breast, and he was going to pay. He was going to pay dearly.

"Help him," Agnes ordered Oliver.

Oliver rushed toward the doc, training his gun on her, its barrel wavering, while Bob lowered his own weapon, tucking it into his belt to free his hands. Then he took a pair of handcuffs from a pack, and began binding Maisy's hands behind her back.

"How did you find us?" Zach asked, keeping his tone conversational.

"We have resources you couldn't even imagine, Mr. Ingram."

Zach looked up as a small airplane passed overhead just then. He remembered seeing a similar aircraft pass over more than once during their journey. So there were more than just the three of them involved in this—this whatever it was. Someone had spotted them, or more likely the horses, from the air.

"And you hiked all this way?" Zach asked.

"Only from our SUV, Mr. Ingram. You took a rather meandering and difficult route. We simply drove, hiked the short distance here and then waited for you to return to the horses. A child could have found you."

The vehicle he'd seen from the hilltop. It was theirs, just as he'd feared.

"And now we will hike back. And you will come along quietly and not make a fuss. If you give me any trouble at all, Mr. Ingram, I'll order Bob to put a bullet in the good doctor's cranium. Do you understand?"

He nodded. "She has nothing to do with any of this. Take me, and let her go."

"I'm afraid that's not possible."

"Then you're going to kill us both, whether we cooperate or not."

"Exactly, Mr. Ingram. I prefer to take you back to the ranch, where we have the means to deal with the cleanup efficiently. But if you force me, I'll see to it you die right here."

He looked her squarely in the eye. "Since I don't want to do anything to make this even a little bit easier or more convenient for you, Agnes, I think I choose the latter. Kill us right here."

Thirteen

Maisy couldn't believe what she was hearing, much less seeing. One minute she was standing there, with Bob at her back about to cuff her hands and Oliver a foot away with a gun pointed at her, and Zach was facing Agnes and her gun barrel. The next minute, Zach's hand shot out to wrench the gun from Agnes with so much force that the woman went stumbling to the ground with a shout. At her cry, Oliver turned his head and his gun in her direction. At that same moment, Zach swung the gun he held toward the trio. Maisy dropped to her knees out of sheer instinct, and he fired.

Behind her, Bob grunted and fell. The horses reared up in alarm, hooves flying. Beside her, Oliver stood still, his gun pointing at nothing. But Zach's was aimed right at him.

"Drop the gun, Oliver," he shouted.

The man did. It thudded to the ground. Behind Zach, Agnes was stirring, and he couldn't watch both directions at once. Maisy scrambled to pick up Oliver's discarded weapon, then hurried to Zach's side, pointing it at Agnes. "Get over there with Oliver," she ordered. Agnes stopped moving, and Maisy saw that she'd closed her hand around a large rock. "Leave it and get up. Now."

Agnes got to her feet, brushed herself off and walked over to where Oliver stood, muttering something about useless assistants.

"Keep your gun on them," Zach told Maisy. "I need to check on Bob."

"Be careful, Zach. He still has a weapon."

He nodded as he moved closer to the large, unmoving lump of humanity. Bob lay facedown in the grass.

Agnes moved and Maisy jerked her attention back where it belonged. "Stay still, dammit!"

"I doubt you even know how to operate that weapon," Agnes challenged.

She was right, but Maisy couldn't let her know that. She shifted the barrel to the far right and squeezed the trigger. The blast was deafening, the recoil so powerful it wrenched her wrist. Again the horses went berserk, their lead ropes pulling loose this time, and they galloped out of sight. Bark flew off a tree far closer to Agnes and Oliver than Maisy had intended. She kept that to herself, though, and simply said, "Think again, Agnes."

Zach had paused halfway to Bob's prone form, his head jerking toward her, but only briefly. He was back to business a moment later, his gun aimed as he nudged the man with the toe of his shoe. "Bob? Wake up. Come on." He nudged again, sighed when there was no response.

Hunkering down, he gripped Bob's shoulder and rolled the man onto his back. Maisy couldn't help but look. And it was a good thing she did. Zach seemed fixated on the hole in Bob's chest, the blood soaking his shirt. He didn't see Bob's left hand rising from the grass, still clutching the gun.

"Zach, look out!"

She immediately swung the gun she held, but hesitated to pull the trigger with Zach so close. He turned, too, spotting Bob's weapon and diving out of the way just as it spat fire. Maisy fired from point-blank range, and Zach rolled in the grass, readying his own firearm.

It wasn't necessary. Maisy's bullet had hit Bob in the head, making a small hole on the way in, and smashing half the skull away on the way out the other side.

She stood there, the gun in her hand, trembling. Then her knees gave way and she sank to the ground.

Suddenly Zach was there, easing the gun from her, tucking it into his waistband. "It's okay. It's okay, Doc, you had no choice."

"I killed him," she whispered. "God, Zach, I *killed* him."

He stroked her hair, but only for a moment. Then he was addressing the other two. "Where are the keys to that vehicle of yours?"

"We left them in the ignition," Agnes said.

"Nice try. Are you going to make me search you?"

Oliver quickly thrust a hand into a pocket and emerged with a set of keys.

"Why are you making it easier on them, you weakling?" Agnes shouted at the old man.

Oliver shot Agnes a look. "They're the ones with the weapons, darling, or haven't you noticed?"

Agnes only sighed and crossed her arms over her chest.

Zach hurried to grab the handcuffs Bob had been about to snap onto Maisy. He took them to Oliver and Agnes. Snapping one end on Agnes's left wrist, he held the gun on her. "Lift your arm up to that tree limb and swing the other cuff over."

She did, scowling at him the entire time.

Zach nodded to Oliver. "Put your right wrist up there and snap that cuff around it."

Oliver did so. Zach double-checked that he'd tightened the cuff, then returned to where Maisy sat on the ground. Her stomach was queasy, her head lighter than it ought to be. She'd sat there watching him, quietly observing everything he did. It was only when he returned to her that she saw the blood on his shoulder. It frightened her enough to knock the shock of having killed a man right out of her body.

She surged to her feet and rushed to him. "Zach, you're bleeding!"

"It's nothing. Bob's shot grazed me. It's fine."

"It's *not*." She tore a strip of cloth from Zach's shirt and tied it tightly around his upper arm and shoulder.

"It'll be okay, Maisy. Now, come on. We have to get out of here."

"He could've killed you," she whispered a moment later.

"He would have if we hadn't done something. It was him or us, Doc. We had no choice here."

"I know that." She stared up into Zach's eyes, seeing more of him than she had before. He'd risked his life to save hers—to save them both.

Zach took their weapons with him when he headed off through the forest.

"They didn't exactly make it tough to find the way, did they?" Maisy asked, keeping close behind him.

The three criminals had beaten a path through the undergrowth. "They probably didn't think there was any reason to. Figured they'd be leading us back in handcuffs, or worse."

She sighed. "I can't seem to grasp how close we just came— I mean, if things had gone differently, we'd have been two lifeless bodies, just lying out there waiting for some hunter to stumble on six months or a year from now."

He paused and turned to study her face. "Try not to dwell on that, Doc. I know it's mind-bending stuff, but it doesn't matter, because it didn't happen. All that matters is now." He put his hands on her shoulders, squeezed them reassuringly. "We're okay now. We're alive."

She pursed her lips and gave him a nod. "I know."

"And we're going to stay that way."

Again she nodded, more firmly this time. Then she looked past him, her brow creasing. "Do you hear something?"

He listened, then listened harder. "Hell, it's that plane that's been flying over."

"Do you suppose he'll be able to tell something went wrong?"

Zach gripped her arm, hurrying them along the path even as he answered. "Let's not stick around long enough to find out."

They walked quickly along the path, until it led to another more defined one, probably an animal trail. When they hit that one, they began to run, because it was fairly clear of debris and worn smooth by time and use.

The plane's engine grew louder. When it passed overhead, Zach grabbed Maisy and pulled her with him to the nearest tree, pressing his body to the bark and seeing her do the same. If they could remain invisible from above...

The plane, a small, yellow crop-duster passed, and they started running again. The trail spilled them onto the logging road, which was also packed, worn earth, only wider. The airplane vanished from sight as soon as it passed over them, because their view of the sky was limited by the density of the forest. However, the airplane's sounds gave them a clear picture of its movements. It continued to move away from them for only a short while, then made a loop and headed back.

"They know something's wrong," Zach said. "They never circled back for a second look before."

The two of them ran full out, and just as the green SUV came into view, the plane passed over them again. Maisy didn't need Zach to tell her what to do this time. She flattened herself to a tree trunk. Zach did, too, hoping the branches forming a canopy over their heads effectively hid them from the airplane.

Again the plane passed. Again they ran, not stopping this time until they reached the vehicle. It was an oversize, four-wheel drive SUV, and its windows were tinted more darkly than Zach thought was probably legal. In fact, it gave him pause, not being able to peer into the vehicle's interior. But only for a moment, because a second later he heard the plane's engine growing louder once more. It had looped around yet again and was coming back for a third look.

He tried the driver's door, but found it locked. As he took out the keys he'd stuffed into his jeans' pocket, the engine grew louder. He jammed a key in the lock, but it didn't fit. He tried the next one, and it did. The plane came closer.

"Hurry, hurry, hurry," Doc whispered beside him. She was practically bouncing up and down.

He turned the key, opened the door, gripped Maisy's arm and helped her in. The plane engine was louder still as he climbed in himself, pulling the door closed at almost the same instant he sensed the plane passing overhead.

Had they been seen? Would it matter? Once the

vehicle began moving, whoever was in the plane would know, anyway.

He used the same key to start the engine, then backed the vehicle around. It wasn't easy, because the SUV was huge and the logging trail narrow. As he got the beast pointed in the opposite direction, he scanned the interior.

No one else was in the vehicle. Zach craned his neck to see the floor of the back seat, and the luggage area behind it. No one was crouching there waiting to jump up and slit his throat, as he'd half feared there might be.

There was a crocheted throw, purple, blue and white, in the far rear. A newspaper and a half-empty bottle of mineral water sat on the back seat. Maisy was using the button on her armrest to lower the window on her side. The moment she did, he could hear the plane again, coming back.

"Hell." He slammed his foot on the gas pedal and they shot forward, back down the logging road that would take them the hell out of there.

The plane soared over them, and this time the hum of the engine was interrupted by the sound of rapid gunfire. Tiny explosions erupted from the ground in front of them, and pinging noises told Zach a few bullets had hit the SUV, even as it bounded down a road never meant for high speeds.

The trees ended abruptly and they shot onto a track bisecting a green field. Stacks of neatly trimmed logs stood to the left, and they zoomed past the pile onto a road. Oil and stone, not asphalt, but a road all the same.

"Where are they?" he asked, glancing at Maisy.

She was looking out the window and up at the sky. "He circled around. He's coming back."

"Get in the rear," he told her. "Climb as far back as you can, Doc. He's aiming for the driver or the engine, both of which are in the front. Go."

"But—"

"*Go.*"

She unfastened her seat belt and climbed into the back. "If he shoots you, I won't be able to control the car from back here."

"Then jump out," he told her. "Stay low. Here he comes."

"Dammit, Zach—"

"Get down!"

She crouched, low enough so he could no longer see her in the rearview mirror. He floored it and veered the car left and right across the road, hoping to make it a little harder for the bullets to hit as the plane flew up behind them. Then, as it sailed over, he hit the brakes suddenly.

The plane raced ahead of them, but the gunman couldn't shoot at them anymore until it circled around and came back. Zach drove as fast as the vehicle would go while the plane circled and returned. It swooped low, bullets flying. He tried the braking strategy again, but this time, once the plane had passed and he pressed the accelerator to the floor, the engine coughed weakly, jerked once or twice and stalled.

Ribbons of smoke and a cloud of steam rose from various holes in the hood. He tried starting it again, but it was no good. Hell.

"We have to get out. Come on." He opened his door, but just as he was getting out he heard a sound like a cell phone bleating.

Maisy scrambled out through the rear door as the plane approached. She met Zach beside the car, gripping his outstretched hand. They were out of time. They ran together toward a large boulder that seemed to him to be the only place to go. The only real cover.

They crouched behind the rock, and Zach fumbled for the guns he'd taken from the others. "Stay very low, Doc. Don't even wiggle. I have an idea."

"You're going to try to shoot them down, aren't you?"

He nodded, watching the sky, a pistol in each hand. "Have you noticed how good you are at reading my mind?"

"With a pair of handguns?" she asked, sounding skeptical. "You're going to shoot at an airplane with a pair of handguns?"

Again he nodded.

"Zach, I think you're letting this hero thing go to your head. Okay, so you saved me from a man twice your size and outsmarted three armed felons. That doesn't mean you can take on a whole machine-gun-equipped airplane all by yourself."

"Tell you the truth, I wouldn't be the least bit tempted to try it if I thought it wasn't our only option." The plane was coming back. He heard it, like a giant, hungry mosquito homing in on blood.

She swallowed loudly, then suddenly he felt a tug at the back of his pants, and realized she had taken the third gun. He glanced back at her. "Maisy, no. Stay down."

"Screw staying down. I can be heroic, too."

The plane soared over the road, bullets peppering the abandoned, crippled SUV. It swooped so low they couldn't have missed it if they'd tried. Zach jumped up and started firing with both guns. Maisy stood beside him, firing in turn. They shot and shot and shot, and all told, it wasn't as hard as Zach had feared it would be. He could see holes appearing in the plane's belly where they fired. And they even had a moment before the gunman inside was able to pinpoint where those shots were coming from.

Zach knew when he did, because a gun barrel turned toward them. He spun, dropping the guns, grabbing Maisy and pushing her down behind the boulder, covering her with his own body as the plane swooped over them, its engine sputtering.

He heard a shout, rose up just a little and saw the plane going down. No one shot at them now, and he and Maisy got up, standing side by side, watching as the nose hit, then one wing, and then the plane cartwheeled and burst into flames, debris exploding in all directions.

They both ducked instinctively. Zach crouched, lifting his arms to shield his face. Maisy kept going, all the way to the ground. She didn't get up again.

Zach frowned, confused until he saw the bloody gash in her head, and the piece of debris lying against the nearby rock. "Doc!" He bent over her, gripped her shoulders, shook her. "Doc, wake up! Come on."

Her head hung limply, eyes moving rapidly beneath her closed lids. "Wake up," he whispered. "Maisy, don't do this. Not now. I haven't even told you that I love you."

There was still no reaction.

He tried to pull himself together, to be logical and effective. To save her. She wasn't bleeding much. Her neck didn't seem to be injured, from what he could tell at least. It had to be the blow to her head. And the only thing he could do to help her was to get her to a hospital as fast as was humanly possible.

He scooped her up in his arms and carried her back to the road, toward the smoking, useless vehicle. He opened the rear door and laid her on the seat. Then he went to the front seat and searched.

"I heard a phone. Dammit, I swear I heard a—"

His voice fell silent as he located the tiny cell phone in a small compartment between the bucket seats. He looked at the readout with a whispered prayer. There was a signal. A weak one, but still…

Zach pressed 9-1-1, then hit Send, raised the phone to his ear and waited.

It seemed an interminable amount of time before a

woman's voice said, "Nine-one-one dispatch, what's your emergency?"

"I have an injured woman. She's taken a blow to the head and she's unconscious. It's bleeding, but not a lot." He rattled off the pertinent facts as efficiently as he could, even as he climbed into the back seat with Maisy, leaning over her, touching her face, willing her to be all right.

"Is she breathing?" the dispatcher asked.

"Yeah. Her heartbeat's kind of slow, but it's steady."

"All right. Good. Where is she right now?"

"She's lying on the back seat of an SUV. The car's disabled, and I have no idea where we are."

"Okay, just stay calm. I want you to look around. Are there any landmarks you can tell me about? Anything that can help us locate you?"

He studied the landscape. "We seem to be on a hillside. The road is oil and stone. A small plane crashed within a few yards of us about ten minutes ago. It was a piece of its debris that hit her. There was an explosion—maybe someone saw it?"

"All right, good. Anything else?"

He racked his brain. "It's the only place so far where I've been able to get cell-phone reception."

"You're calling from a cell phone?"

"Yes, ma'am."

"Perfect. Just leave it on. We'll trace the signal." She spoke to someone else, her voice muffled, then came back on the line with him. "Can you tell me what happened, sir?"

He thought about that. Could he? Could he tell the dispatcher that he had been kidnapped, drugged, tortured? That they'd escaped on stolen horses, only to face three armed killers in a standoff deep in the forest? That they'd wrested the guns from the bad guys, left them bound in the woods and stolen their vehicle, only to be peppered with gunfire from an airplane? That they'd shot that airplane down with handguns?

"Sir?" she prodded. "Can you tell me what happened?"

"Not without convincing you that I'm totally insane, no. But you'd probably better send the police along with that ambulance. If you guys can trace a cell-phone signal, I have no doubt other people can, too."

"Other people?"

"Just hurry."

"They're on the way, sir."

Forty-five minutes passed liked forty-five days, but they passed all the same. The police arrived, and Zach told them his story. They might have concluded he was nuts if not for the bullet-ridden SUV bearing silent witness, along with the still-smoking airplane. One cop checked out the wreckage, but came back shaking his head.

"Two bodies inside, I think. Too charred to identify, probably. And I think there's an automatic weapon in the rubble there, but it's too hot to get close enough to be sure. Better wait for a fire company to hose this thing down so we can gather evidence.''

The older cop nodded and continued patting Zach down.

Zach told him about the guns, all of which were in the back of the SUV, where he'd put them when he'd heard the sirens approaching. No sense making the cops nervous. He also told them about Oliver and Agnes and the late Bob, and where he'd left them in the woods, two bound, one dead.

He didn't think they believed him entirely. The more he talked, the more downright amazed looks the two cops exchanged. But they couldn't disbelieve him, either.

The ambulance arrived, and EMTs quickly went to work on Maisy. Zach never took his eyes off her. As paramedics took her vital signs, started an IV, slid a backboard underneath her and strapped her to it.

When they lifted the backboard onto a gurney and began rolling her toward the ambulance, Zach turned to follow.

''Wait, now,'' said the older cop, whose name tag said Dillon. ''We can't just let you go off. You're going to have to come to the station with us until we can verify your story.''

Zach paused, turning back to him. ''Look, my brother is Jake Ingram,'' he said. ''He's working with the FBI on the World Bank heist. It's been all over the papers. I'm sure you've read about it.''

Officer Dillon sent the younger cop, Sprague, a look, then focused on Zach again. ''Then you're the Zachary Ingram who's been missing from Greenlaurel these past few days?''

''Yes. That's me. But it was Jake these idiots were after. They grabbed the wrong brother. I'm the victim in all this. I need to warn Jake. And I need to go to the hospital with that woman. If you want to put me in handcuffs and leg irons and send an armed officer along with me, do it. Do whatever you have to. But I'm going with her. I can't lose her. Not now.''

The cops exchanged glances, and Dillon nodded. ''You can go. My partner, Officer Sprague, will go along. Tom, you ride up front with the driver. Put in a call to Jake Ingram to verify this guy is who he says he is, and stay with him at the hospital until you hear different. I'll check out the woods where he said he left those other people.''

The younger cop nodded, started for the ambulance. Zach did, too, but then he paused, turning to the older man again. ''Officer Dillon?''

The cop spun around.

''Don't go out there alone. These people…they're ruthless. They're smart. And I get the feeling they're…''

''They're what, son?''

''Organized. I think there's a lot more to this than

just those three out there and whoever was in that airplane. A lot more. If you walk out there alone, I don't know how many might be out there waiting for you.''

Fourteen

The hospital was a half hour away, in a town so small it probably didn't even appear on the map. The medics rolled Maisy through a pair of double doors, while the younger cop, Officer Tom Sprague, and a couple of nurses, hustled Zach into a small waiting area.

Zach could see into the hallway, and to the double doors at the end of it, which were sort of kitty-corner from the waiting area. They were closed, and he couldn't see a thing beyond them. His heart hurt, literally ached. He'd never felt a sensation like that before—worry, fear, utter dread manifesting as physical pain. It was damned odd.

He supposed that was what love did to a man.

He looked at the pay phone on the far wall of the waiting room. "Officer Sprague? Did you manage to reach my brother?"

"I had the dispatcher contact him. He's on his way here now."

Zach sighed, but felt no rush of relief. The ordeal wasn't over. Not until Maisy Jane Dalton came out of that E.R. with a smile on her face and a clean bill of health.

"Say, you should have that looked at," the cop said suddenly.

Zach glanced down at his shoulder, where a little fresh blood had decided to put in an appearance. "I kind of forgot."

"I assumed that was her blood on your arm before," he said, then went to the doorway and said, "Hey, nurse, this guy's bleeding in here. Can we get him some help?"

The nurse came hurrying into the room, frowning at his shoulder as she lifted the sleeve.

"It's nothing," he said. "How's Maisy doing?"

"I don't know anything yet, other than that this is a nasty wound and it needs attention. Now you just come with me."

He didn't argue. The cop followed as the nurse, a rail-thin bleached blonde whose face showed signs of age, even if her hair and body didn't, led Zach into a treatment room. She had him perched on a table and shirtless within a few seconds. Then she went to work cleaning the wound, making him suck air through his teeth. She shook her head slowly. "This needs stitching."

"Just slap a bandage on it."

"When was your last tetanus shot, Mr. Ingram?"

"I teach at a university. They make sure I'm up to date on every immunization and booster ever invented."

She nodded. "It should still be stitched."

"I won't consent."

"Men are too stubborn."

He looked at the woman. She rolled her eyes and reached for some bandages. When she had the thing wrapped, he slid off the table, pulled on his shirt and walked out of the room, ignoring the nurse's instructions on keeping the wound clean, applying antibiotic ointment and changing the dressing. He knew how to care for a scratch, thank you.

All he was interested in was seeing how Maisy was doing, and now that he'd escaped the waiting room, maybe he could get a glance. He hurried to the room where they'd taken her, reached out and pushed open the doors.

People surrounded the table where she was lying—doctors, nurses. He couldn't even see her, except for one, pale slender hand hanging off the side of the table.

"She's in V-fib!"

"Gimme 200 amps. Ready? Clear!"

They backed away from the table, all but one man, who held two paddles to Maisy's chest. There was a dull, thudding pulse of sound, and Maisy's body arched off the table, then landed again.

"Mr. Ingram, you have to—"

He shook the cop's hand off his shoulder and watched.

"Again. Three hundred! Clear!"

The doctor shocked Maisy again. Her back arched, relaxed. Zach felt tears burning his eyes, and he shouted, "Dammit, Maisy, don't give up. Not now.

You know perfectly well we've got unfinished business!''

"Again! Clear!''

"Maisy, come back!'' Zach shouted.

"Someone get him out of here,'' the doctor ordered, pausing with his paddles in the air as the machine hummed.

"Doctor, wait,'' someone said. "I'm getting a rhythm.''

All eyes turned toward the little screen with its neon-green lines and irritating tones. The lines were jumping, spiking, where before they'd been wavering and nearly flat. The spikes became more regular, stronger, and Zach knew enough to understand what that meant.

He lowered his head. "I'm here, Maisy. I'm waiting for you right here,'' he said.

Another hand lowered onto his shoulder. He turned, but this time it wasn't the cop standing behind him. It was his brother. It was Jake.

Jake didn't say anything. He just put his arms around Zach, clapping him on the shoulders as he hugged him, briefly but powerfully. Zach winced, and Jake let go, stepping back and glancing down at the bloodstained shirtsleeve. Then he looked at Zach's unshaved face.

"God, you look like you've been through hell.''

"You don't know the half of it.'' Zach turned to look through the mesh-lined glass again. The doctors and nurses surrounding Maisy seemed calmer now, and the machine was beeping at a steady pace.

"She someone special, Zach?"

"More than I think she knows." Convinced Maisy was past the crisis point, Zach sighed and, turning, led his brother into the waiting area. "She saved my life, that woman in there."

"Maybe you'd better start from the beginning."

"That would probably be less confusing." He sank into a vinyl chair, closed his eyes. Jake went to one of the vending machines and when he came back he handed a hot foam cup to Zach. Zach sipped. "Cocoa?"

"Yeah. Anything's better than machine-brewed coffee."

"Good decision."

"So?"

"So I came out of class, and this harmless-looking little old lady pulled up in a car and asked for assistance. I started to talk with her, and a big guy came up behind me and jabbed me in the arm with a hypodermic needle. Next thing I knew, I was strapped to a bed in a farmhouse, surrounded by strangers who kept calling me Jake."

Jake frowned hard.

"Do you have any clue what this could be about?" Zach asked his brother.

Jake shook his head. "I had an anonymous note from someone claiming to have information I needed. I was supposed to meet her in the park last night, but she never showed. I was still there waiting when the sun came up this morning." He frowned. "And that's just between us, brother. But go on. What else happened?"

Zach sighed. "They gave me regular doses of Sodium Pentothal. Of course, I didn't know what it was until later. They shone blindingly bright lights into my eyes and asked me questions I couldn't begin to answer. Stuff about my childhood, my brothers and sisters, my parents. And in between all that, they would read me nursery rhymes."

"Nursery rhymes?"

He nodded. "Crazy, I know. 'Jack and Jill went up the hill' and 'The cow jumped over the moon' and 'Pussycat, pussycat, where have you been—'"

"'I've been to London, to look at the queen,'" Jake said, his voice deep and a little bit off-key. Zach frowned at him as he continued. "'Pussycat, pussycat, what did you there? I frightened a mouse from under her chair.'"

"Jake?"

Jake blinked, and seemed to shake himself. "I... Sorry. I know that one from...somewhere."

Zach set his cocoa aside, sat up straighter, studying his brother, the faraway look in his eyes, the expression that told him something was on Jake's mind. Something besides the here and now. And given the matter at hand, it must be something big.

"Jake, it's obvious to me they were after you. They thought I was you. And I'm afraid they'll try again."

He nodded, not even arguing.

"I imagine it has something to do with the World Bank heist," Zach said.

"It might. But I don't know, Zach. I don't know. I think there might be...something else."

"Like what?"

Jake shrugged, paced away. "Lately I've been having those dreams again, only more intense than before. Almost like...memories. There's a man, a big bear of a man, running and playing with a pile of kids on the beach. And then there's this woman—this gentle, beautiful young woman. There are a bunch of kids, and I'm one of them, and I smell violets all the time—" He broke off there, shaking himself and focusing once more on Zach. "Listen to me, going on about odd dreams, when you're in the freaking hospital. How did you get away from those maniacs, anyway?"

Zach was worried about his brother, and something he'd said set off alarm bells, but he'd think about that later. He looked toward the E.R., the room where they were still working on Maisy. "It was her, Dr. Maisy Jane Dalton. They lured her out there by telling her I was their long-lost nephew, that I'd been brainwashed by some cult. She's a shrink, an expert in hypnosis and deprogramming. So she bought it, and went out there."

Jake frowned even harder. "So they thought they had me, and they brought in a deprogrammer to get me to tell them something?"

"Yeah. Something about your past. Your childhood." Zach snapped his fingers. "And they used violet-scented oil in the room where they kept me. Geez, Jake, this has to have something to do with your past. But how can that be related to the World Bank heist?"

"I don't know. Keep talking, maybe we'll find the connection."

Zach shook his head slowly. "I was able to convince Maisy that I wasn't who they thought I was. She found the drug stash, and substituted saline for the Pentothal. We let them keep injecting me, and I played it up, but in truth we were giving my head time to clear and my strength to come back, so we could escape."

"Then she was a prisoner, too?"

Zach nodded. "They rigged her car with explosives. If she'd tried to use it to get away, she'd have been blown to bits. The phone lines were out, too. We planned to leave in the dead of night. Take some supplies with us. But we ran out of time."

"Why?" Jake asked.

"The thug who was left to guard us decided to attack the doc. Knocked her around a little. I think he would have raped her, but I came in and clocked him over the head. He turned on me instead and I managed to be the one left standing."

Jake was staring at his brother, a smile of admiration touching his lips. "I always knew you had it in you."

"I didn't."

"Then you're not as smart as I thought." He shook his head. "So then you ran."

"Yeah, we took two horses and rode off. They caught up with us again in the woods, though. We fought again. I almost got my head blown off that time, but the doc fired first. Killed the thug. I handcuffed the other two and left them in the woods. We took their SUV, but then someone was after us in a small aircraft, and they were firing at us with a machine gun."

"The police said you two shot the plane down with nothing but handguns."

Zach nodded. "It wasn't as impressive as it sounds. The plane was just a crop-duster, and it was swooping so low, it would have been hard to miss. The plane exploded on impact, and a piece of debris hit the doc." He looked toward the E.R. again. "It hit her hard, Jake. Right in the head." He sighed softly. "I found a cell phone in the truck and called 9-1-1, and that's about it."

Officer Dillon came in from the opposite side of the waiting room, his hat in his hand. "How's she doing, Mr. Ingram?"

"We still don't know," Zach said. Then, remembering himself, he added, "This is my brother, Jake Ingram. Jake, this is Officer Dillon. He was the first one to get to us out there."

The officer nodded as Jake shook his hand. "Do you have any identification on you, Mr. Ingram?"

"Certainly." Jake took out his wallet, handed the man his driver's license and waited while he inspected it.

Nodding, the cop handed it back. "And I take it you can verify that this man is indeed your brother, Zachary Ingram?"

"Absolutely."

Again the cop nodded. "I could tell by looking at you, but I had to ask for the record."

"What happened with the search?" Zach asked. "Did you find those three in the woods?"

The cop licked his lips. "It's the damnedest thing, but no. Not a sign of them. Not even the one you believed had been killed. Not a footprint, not a speck of blood. We did find those two horses, though, running loose out there. But that was all."

"Then they got away," Zach said. He turned his eyes on Jake. "And if they're organized enough to make every scrap of evidence disappear, they're even more dangerous than I feared. They're still out there, and I'd bet money they're still after you."

"Right now, I'm spending my days with a federal agent, and my nights with my fiancée, who's twice as intimidating. Don't worry about me." Jake held his brother's gaze, and the humor faded from his eyes. "I'm sorry, Zach. I'm so damn sorry you and that innocent woman in there got dragged into this mess because of me. I was at the university just last week, remember?"

Zach nodded. "As a guest lecturer."

"They must have seen me there, maybe they were following me even then. I don't know. They obviously took you because of me."

"Not because of you, Jake. None of this was your fault, not in any way."

Jake lowered his eyes, and Zach knew he disagreed. But before he could work any harder to reassure his brother, he saw those double doors open. Maisy was wheeled out on a stretcher, tubes in her arms and up her nose, wire leads on her chest, and only a thin sheet covering her.

He raced forward, but a doctor stepped into his path. "We should talk."

"I want to see her."

"In a few minutes. They're taking her to a room now, getting her settled in."

"I'm not sure that's such a good idea," Zach said, glancing at Jake.

Jake agreed. "He's right. She should be moved to Greenlaurel. I can have the feds put guards on her room until she's well again."

The doctor looked away so fast it made Zach's heart compress. "Doctor?" he asked. "She *is* going to be well again, isn't she?"

Forcing his gaze to meet Zach's, the doctor sighed. "The truth is, we don't know. Her heart stopped once—not uncommon with a severe head injury. We got it started again, but she's in a coma, son. Right now it's impossible to say whether she'll even come out of it at all. And we can't even begin to make an assessment of her prognosis until she does. I'm sorry.''

Maisy was floating. There was no pain. Only warmth and comfort. She liked where she was. She remembered, vaguely, the sharpness and pain of what had come before. Everything had been too bright. Too hard. Too harsh. This new place was different. Things were muted and beautiful, soothing and soft. Safe. She felt, above all else, safe there.

Michael was there. She became aware of him slowly, gradually, and when she turned toward him, she didn't see him with her eyes, exactly. It was more like a shifting presence in her mind, glowing and beautiful. He held out his hand toward her.

She smiled, remembering that it had always been this way with Michael. Comfortable, soft, *safe*.

Until the end. Michael had brought danger and risk into their safe haven, and destroyed it forever.

Without a word, he told her it was all right. That he'd found peace again. That there was nothing but peace where he was now. He reached out a hand to her, offering her peace, too.

She hesitated, because there was something else, something she was forgetting.

''Doc, you need to wake up now.''

The voice came from a great distance. But it was a familiar voice, a beloved one. It made her heart leap in her chest and her pulse quicken.

"Do you hear me, Doc? Come on. Come back to me now."

The image of Michael, the sense of him, faded into the mists, and she turned and searched for that voice. Zach. Yes, she remembered now.

"Come on, Maisy Jane Dalton, wake up. I know you can do it."

She frowned, because his voice, when she tried to follow it, brought other things with it. First, there was an intense and growing brightness that hurt her eyes. There were feelings—not the mundane, comfortable, dull feelings Michael had brought with him, but powerful, shattering feelings. There was fear. Someone was after her back there, after both of them. There was attraction and longing so intense she ached with it. There was horrible uncertainty, accompanied by the crushing weight of a thousand decisions to be made, suddenly bearing down on her shoulders. And there was fire, fire so hot it could consume her.

She stopped moving toward Zach, instead turning and looking for Michael again.

He appeared as soon as she thought of him, but he was farther away this time. Still, he held out his hand, and when she thought about taking it, the harsh light faded, along with the other feelings.

"Doc, come on now. We said we'd give this thing a chance. We can't very well do that if you don't come back to me, can we?"

A hand brushed along her neck. It brought that familiar fire with it. It burned, inside and out, hotter than the comfortable warmth of this place, of Michael. It tingled inside her. Her heart pounded and she gasped for breath. It was too intense, too dangerous. She turned to see that hand, the man she knew was touching her, but there was no one there. She could feel him, but she couldn't see him.

"That's it, Doc. You're trying, I can tell you're trying. Come back to me. Come on."

She wanted to. But God, she wasn't certain she could bear it. The light had returned now, blindingly bright. And the return of physical sensation, which seemed to have been instigated by his invisible touch, brought pain with it. Pounding, splitting pain that pulsed in her head like a jackhammer.

She panted, trying to breathe. There were sounds, steady beeps and tones, and voices that hurt her ears. There were smells, something harsh that made her wrinkle her nose. It was too much!

Once more she turned to look back at Michael, standing in the muted pastel light that didn't hurt her, with his gentle touch that didn't ignite her soul, in a place where soft mists blocked pain and worry, and no decisions needed to be made, beyond just the one—the one to go there. There was no risk there; her senses could rest, blanketed and safe.

"Maisy, you have to fight," Zach's voice whispered to her, and when his hands touched her again, she felt herself tremble. "I know it's hard, but you have to do it anyway. Come on, fight your way back to me, Doc. I need you here. I—I love you, you know.''

Michael took a step backward, and then the mists swallowed him up. He was gone, and the mists were retreating.

She'd made up her mind. She had to go back.

Maisy turned again toward the world of the physical. Of blinding light, harsh, earsplitting sounds and acrid smells, and the pain of her wounded body. She couldn't hear him anymore. And she was lost in sensation too potent to bear.

''Zach!'' she cried.

Fifteen

Zach had been by Maisy's side day and night, for the nearly sixty-two hours since she had been moved by ambulance to Greenlaurel Community Hospital. He took his meals in the chair beside her bed. He used the bathroom attached to her hospital room when he had to, and as quickly as he could manage. He had shaved, though he hadn't wanted to be away from her long enough to do that. Only when Jake was there to watch over Maisy did Zach pry himself away long enough to shower and brush his teeth. He didn't want her alone, and having a guard outside the door wasn't good enough.

He'd been talking to her constantly, trying to keep her from slipping any further away from him. Trying to make her come back. He'd been hopeful a few times, when the slow, steady tone of her heart monitor picked up as if in reaction to his voice, or when the numbers on her blood pressure readout started climbing higher. Her breathing would increase, and this last time she'd even begun moving her head back and forth on the pillows.

But this time, like every other time he thought he was making progress, it ended abruptly. The monitors slowed back down, she grew still in the bed and her breathing slowed.

Devastated for the umpteenth time, Zach sighed softly, letting himself feel the disappointment only for a moment, before vowing silently that he would not give up. He got to his feet, walked slowly toward the door, intending to send someone to the cafeteria for fresh coffee.

He was at the door, his hand pulling it open, when he heard Maisy say, very clearly, "Zach!"

He froze for just an instant, then turned around.

She still lay there, and her eyes were closed, but she wasn't calm. Her body began thrashing around on the bed, and her arms swung wildly. She hit the IV pole, knocking it sideways.

Zach lunged, caught the pole, then bent over her, capturing her wrists in his hands. "Maisy, it's okay. It's okay, I'm here." He had to speak loudly to be sure she could hear him over the rapid-fire beeping of her heart monitor. She felt damp with sweat and was trembling, fighting him.

"I'm here, I'm here, I'm right here."

She stilled all at once. Her arms went limp as he held them, and her breath sighed out of her as her heart rate began to slow again.

Zach battled a fresh round of disappointment as he let go of her wrists and reached up to smooth her hair out of her eyes.

Her *open* eyes.

"Maisy?" He cupped her cheeks with his palms. "Doc, are you awake? Can you hear me?"

Her brows drew into a tight frown, and her eyelids narrowed to a squint. "Lights..."

"Lights? Okay, okay, honey, I've got them." He reached to the pull-cord above the bed, tugged it until the bright light over her head went out. "Better?"

"Noise," she whispered, her face still screwed up tight.

"All right, okay." He turned to the monitor, found a volume control on it and lowered it as far as it would go. The steady *beep-beep* faded to silence. Then he searched her face again.

Maisy sighed, her face relaxing just a little. "Pain," she told him.

"I'll make them give you something for that." He reached past her to hit the call button that lay near her pillow.

Swallowing hard, she nodded. "I heard you calling me," she whispered. "I came back."

"I'm glad." He sat on the edge of her bed, holding her hand in his own. "You have no idea how glad I am."

"It was like...it was like a cocoon. Warm and... safe. I liked it there, except..." She frowned as if puzzled.

"Except what?" he asked.

Her frown eased then, as if the answer had come to her. "You weren't there."

Zach's throat tightened in a way it had seldom

done, and his eyes felt suspiciously hot and damp. He didn't have time to say more to her, though, because a nurse came through the door, took one look at the two of them and then hit the call box on the wall. "Page Dr. Wallace. The patient is awake."

A muted voice came over the P.A. system immediately. "Dr. Wallace to room two-nineteen stat."

"You're gonna have to wait outside, Mr. Ingram," the nurse said, even as two others hurried into the room to join them. "We need to check her over."

Zach nodded, pressing a kiss to Maisy's hand, feeling his belly knot up at the panic that showed in her eyes when she whispered, "Don't go."

"I'm going to be right outside that door," he told her. "Not one inch farther, and I'll come right back in the second the doctor finishes examining you."

Tears spilled over, and she held his hand, refusing to let go. "No. Don't go!"

"All right now, Maisy, take it easy," the nurse said. "How about if we just have Mr. Ingram wait over there by the window, hmm? Would that be okay?"

Her bottom lip was trembling as she nodded to the nurse, never taking her eyes from Zach's. He had never felt more needed or more loved than he did then. Never, not in his entire life.

He kissed her knuckles again, and this time she eased her grip. Then he slipped his hand out of hers, walked over to the chair by the window and sat down.

But he held her gaze with his eyes the entire time, promising silently not to let go.

Vowing in his heart not to *ever* let her go.

Maisy couldn't take her eyes from Zach's, and she wasn't sure why. Maybe it was the odd notion that if she looked away, even for a moment, she would lose him forever. Or perhaps it was the sudden realization that she didn't *want* to lose him—ever—that kept her eyes glued to his.

A nurse said she would inject her with something to ease Maisy's pain, but not until the doctor finished his thorough exam. He tested her reflexes, asked her questions, tickled the bottoms of her feet, made her touch her nose, looked into her eyes with a tiny light and did a dozen other things before he finally nodded at the nurse to give her the shot.

By then the pain was thrumming mercilessly in Maisy's head. It hurt so badly her eyes were watering as they clung to Zach's worried stare. But still she hesitated, jerking her arm away when the nurse bent over it with the needle. "It's not going to make me sleep, is it?" she asked.

"It might."

"Then don't give it to me. I don't want to go back to sleep." As she said it, her eyes held Zach's, and even in her own mind the words were filled with meaning. She wondered if Zach knew, if he understood. How could he, though, when she was only beginning to comprehend it herself?

"It'll help the pain, dear."

"No." She made her voice firm this time, even managed to look at the nurse when she said it. "Do *not* inject me with that."

Blinking in surprise, the nurse backed away, glancing at the doctor with a question in her eyes.

He nodded and scribbled a note on Maisy's chart. "I'll have her get you some Tylenol with codeine, instead. It'll at least take the edge off. All right?"

Maisy nodded.

"Now there are some officers who want to talk to you. They've been waiting a long time."

"They can wait a little longer," she said, sending the doctor a plea with her eyes. "Can't they?"

He glanced from her to Zach, then nodded in understanding. "I'll give you an hour. But then I'm going to have to let them in." And with that, he went to the door, opened it and inclined his head at the nurses. One by one they filed out, and he followed them, closing the door behind him.

Maisy turned her head, though it hurt to move, and sought out Zach. He was already on his way to her again, already closing his hand around hers, leaning over to press his cool, gentle lips to her throbbing head.

"I don't want to sleep anymore, Zach," she told him.

"I know."

"No. No, you don't."

Zach straightened so he could stare down at her. "Then tell me."

She nodded. "I've been sleeping my way through life ever since Michael died. I've been hiding in a place, a place very much like the one I've been in since that airplane exploded." She frowned. "How long was I there, Zach?"

He closed his eyes as if the memory pained him. "Three days. You've been a coma for three days now, Doc. I was so afraid for you."

"Oh, but there was no reason to be. It was nice there. A soft, safe, warm place where I couldn't feel anything. No pain, no fear, no worry. I saw Michael."

Zach frowned, studying her.

"He wanted me to come with him into that safe place, to stay there. But then I heard you. You were calling me back."

"You could hear me?"

She nodded, and the movement hurt, causing her to wince. Zach pressed his hand to her forehead, gently urging her to lie back on the pillows.

She breathed, tried to relax. "I heard you," she said softly. "And I started to come back, but things got harder, harsher and brighter. I could feel pain and fear again. All the things that didn't exist in that other world. And I think that's when I realized it wasn't just there, in that misty place, that I couldn't feel. I've been living in a place just like it. Isolated from everything that could hurt me, completely cut off from any possibility of pain. But in hiding myself from hurt, I hid myself from life, too. Zach, I hadn't felt alive, truly alive, since Michael died. Not until I walked into that bedroom at that stupid ranch and looked into your eyes for the first time.''

He smiled softly. ''When I opened my eyes and saw you there, I thought you were an angel. And as soon as I realized you were an actual woman, and that I was alive, I felt this…swelling in my chest. I think I fell in love with you right then, Maisy. Drugs and all, I fell. One look at those eyes, and I was gone. I just— I didn't think it would be wise to tell you.''

''I was so afraid of you,'' she told him. ''I was so afraid of what I felt, because it meant I had to risk being hurt again.''

''There's no hurt without risk, that's true,'' he told her. ''But there's no joy, either. No passion, no pleasure. It's a package deal.''

''I know. I know that now.''

''I'll never hurt you the way he did,'' he whispered. ''I can promise you that, Maisy. I can't imagine even wanting to look at any other woman, not if I have you.'' He paused, lowered his eyes. ''Do I? Have you, I mean?'' Then he shook his head. ''I'm pushing you too fast. I know, you were afraid our…our feelings were based on the situation, the danger we were in. You wanted to spend some time in the real world, make sure we still—''

Maisy pressed a forefinger to his lips, silencing him. ''I do want to spend time with you in the real world,'' she said. ''But not to make sure our feelings are real. I already know they are. So real they pulled me out of a coma. So real they brought me back to life. Yes, Zach. You *do* have me. I love you.''

He leaned in, gathered her into his arms so gently it was as if he feared she might break. And then he kissed her.

And that was when Maisy Jane Dalton's life began.

* * * * *

*There are more secrets to reveal—
don't miss out!
Coming in July 2003 to
Silhouette Books.*

*She always knew she was different,
but could her life really be a*

PYRAMID OF LIES
by
Anne Marie Winston

*Family Secrets: Five extraordinary
siblings. One dangerous past.
Unlimited potential.*

*And now,
for a sneak peek,
just turn the page…*

Gretchen Wagner didn't even know her true birth date. How pathetic was that?

Her adoptive parents had celebrated her birthday on Valentine's Day, saying they had gotten their heart's desire the day they adopted Gretchen, but after their respective deaths, she'd found her adoption papers. Except for the year, 1967, the actual date had been left blank, as had any reference to her biological parents. It was almost as if she had never existed before the day they'd brought her home. Which she knew couldn't be true.

She'd had a dozen years of life before her adoption. For some reason that no doctor had ever been able to discern, her memory of her childhood before that point was limited to a hazy image of a pretty dark-haired woman—her mother?—and a wide stretch of sandy beach with gentle waves that frothed onto the shore in endlessly mesmerizing, rolling breakers.

Those memories had been with her always, and she generally dismissed them. Her adoption had been private and there were no records left to pursue even if she had wanted to find her birth parents. Which she didn't. After more than two decades, what would be the point? Obviously, her memory loss was from some physical or emotional trauma stemming from a childhood spent with those parents. The beach...who knew? A vacation memory, perhaps? For Gretchen, the bottom line was that she'd been adopted by two warm, gentle people who made her feel safe and loved. What would be the point in subjecting herself to possibly years of therapy to try to recover memories that might be better left buried?

She began to read the menu the server had handed her, and as she did so, a shadow fell across her table.

"Good evening."

That voice! She felt a tingle of instant recognition as she looked up. It was, as she'd known, the stranger from the elevator. She immediately began to blush furiously.

He didn't appear to notice. "Are you waiting for someone?"

She shook her head and cleared her throat. "Ah...no."

The man smiled and extended his hand. "I'm Kurt Miller. From Austin, Texas. May I join you for dinner?"

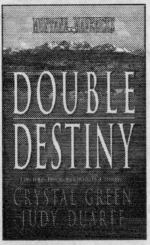

**Like a spent wave,
washing broken shells back to sea,
the clues to a long-ago death had been
caught in the undertow of time...**

Coming in
July 2003

Undertow

Cold cases were
Gray Hollowell's specialty,
and for a bored detective
on disability, turning over
clues from a twenty-seven-
year-old boating fatality
on exclusive Henry Island
was just the vacation he
needed. Edgar Henry had
paid him cash, given him
the keys to his cottage, told him what he knew about
his wife's death—then up and died. But it wasn't until
Edgar's vulnerable daughter, Mariah, showed up to
scatter Edgar's ashes that Gray felt the pull of her
innocent beauty—and the chill of this cold case.

Only from Silhouette Books!

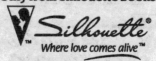

In June 2003

Silhouette Books
invites you to share
a blessed event

Baby Love

She had promised to raise her sister's baby
as her own, with no interference from the baby's
insufferable father. But that was before she met
that darkly handsome, if impossible, man! He was
someone she was having a hard time ignoring.
Don't miss Joan Elliott Pickart's *Mother at Heart*.

Their passionate marriage was over,
their precious dreams in ashes.
And then a swelling in her belly made
one couple realize that one of their dreams
would yet see the light of day.
Look for Victoria Pade's *Baby My Baby*.

Available at your favorite retail outlet.

Where love comes alive™

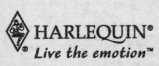
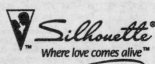

Silhouette®
Where love comes alive™

FAMILY SECRETS

Five extraordinary siblings.
One dangerous past.
Unlimited potential.

Collect four (4) original proofs of purchase from the back pages of four (4) Family Secrets titles and receive a specialty themed free gift valued at over $20.00 U.S.!

Just complete the order form and send it, along with four (4) proofs of purchase from four (4) different Family Secrets titles to: Family Secrets, P.O. Box 9047, Buffalo, NY 14269-9047, or P.O. Box 613, Fort Erie, Ontario L2A 5X3.

Name (PLEASE PRINT)

Address   Apt. #

City   State/Prov.   Zip/Postal Code

Please specify which themed gift package(s) you would like to receive:

❑ PASSION
❑ HOME AND FAMILY
❑ TENDER AND LIGHTHEARTED

❑ Have you enclosed your proofs of purchase?

One Proof Of Purchase FSPOP1

Remember—for each package selected, you must send four (4) original proofs of purchase. To receive all three (3) gifts, just send in twelve (12) proofs of purchase, one from each of the 12 Family Secrets titles.

Please allow 4-6 weeks for delivery. Shipping and handling included. Offer good only while quantities last. Offer available in Canada and the U.S. only. Request should be received no later than July 31, 2004. Each proof of purchase should be cut out of the back page ad featuring this offer.

Visit us at www.eHarlequin.com   FSPOP1